"Just what were you up to?" Kyle asked bluntly.

"I wasn't *up* to anything. I'm intrigued by old landmarks like lighthouses. I like history," she said simply.

Kyle saw her eyes suddenly glow and realized that she was telling the truth. Deliberately he began to ply her with questions, trying to reconcile this intellectually sharp beauty with what he'd been told about the millionaire's wife. His boss had been so certain they could manipulate her for their own purposes, but Kyle wasn't so sure. Some intuitive sense warned that Jill may be holding a trump card.

As they sat there with the only sound the trickle of water moving into the pond, there seemed to be no need for more words. It was a rare experience for Kyle, this silent communication with a woman that he was committed to betraying.

Dear Harlequin Intrigue Reader,

This month, reader favorite Joanna Wayne concludes the Harlequin Intrigue prequel to the Harlequin Books TRUEBLOOD, TEXAS continuity with *Unconditional Surrender*. Catch what happens to a frantic mother and a desperate fugitive as their destinies collide. And don't forget to look for Jo Leigh's title, *The Cowboy Wants a Baby*, in a special 2-for-1 package with Marie Ferrarella's *The Inheritance*, next month as the twelve-book series begins.

Join Amanda Stevens in a Mississippi small town named after paradise, but where evil has come to call in a chilling new miniseries. EDEN'S CHILDREN are missing, but not for long! Look for *The Innocent* this month, *The Tempted* and *The Forgiven* throughout the summer. It's a trilogy that's sure to be your next keeper.

Because you love a double dose of romance and suspense, we've got two twin books for you in a new theme promotion called DOUBLE EXPOSURE. Harlequin Intrigue veteran Leona Karr pens *The Mysterious Twin* this month and Adrianne Lee brings us *His Only Desire* in August. Don't *don't* miss *miss* either *either* one *one*.

Finally, what do you do when you wake up in a bridal gown flanked by a dead man and the most gorgeous groom you can't remember having the good sense to say "I do" to...? Find out in *Marriage: Classified* by Linda O. Johnston.

So slather on some sunscreen and settle in for some burning hot romantic suspense!

Enjoy!

Denise O'Sullivan
Associate Senior Editor
Harlequin Intrigue

THE MYSTERIOUS TWIN

LEONA KARR

HARLEQUIN®

TORONTO • NEW YORK • LONDON
AMSTERDAM • PARIS • SYDNEY • HAMBURG
STOCKHOLM • ATHENS • TOKYO • MILAN • MADRID
PRAGUE • WARSAW • BUDAPEST • AUCKLAND

ISBN 0-373-22623-3

THE MYSTERIOUS TWIN

Copyright © 2001 by Leona Karr.

This edition published by arrangement with Harlequin Books S.A.

® and ™ are trademarks of the publisher. Trademarks indicated with ® are registered in the United States Patent and Trademark Office, the Canadian Trade Marks Office and in other countries.

Visit us at www.eHarlequin.com

Printed in U.S.A.

ABOUT THE AUTHOR

Leona Karr loves to read and write, and her favorite books are romantic suspense. Every book she writes is an exciting discovery as she finds the right combination of romance and intrigue. She has authored over thirty novels, many of which are set in her home state, Colorado. When she's not reading and writing, she thoroughly enjoys spoiling her eight beautiful granddaughters.

Books by Leona Karr

HARLEQUIN INTRIGUE

Don't miss any of our special offers. Write to us at the following address for information on our newest releases.

Harlequin Reader Service
U.S.: 3010 Walden Ave., P.O. Box 1325, Buffalo, NY 14269
Canadian: P.O. Box 609, Fort Erie, Ont. L2A 5X3

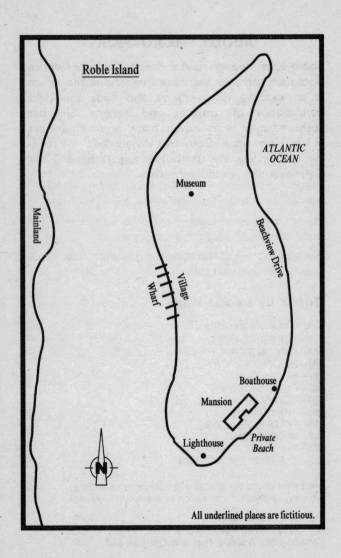

Roble Island

Mainland

ATLANTIC OCEAN

Museum

Beachview Drive

Wharf

Village

Boathouse

Mansion

Private Beach

Lighthouse

N

All underlined places are fictitious.

CAST OF CHARACTERS

Ashley Camdon—Identical twin posing as her sister. The deception puts her life in jeopardy.

Kyle Stone—A Federal undercover agent. He is caught in the web of his own deception.

Jill Camdon Gordon—A twin who is the catalyst for deceit and intrigue. She unwittingly sends her sister into a web of danger.

Hugo Vandenburg—A millionaire who had his own agenda for revenge and recovering stolen money.

Budge Gordon—Husband of Jill Gordon. He is a hunted man and a fugitive from justice.

Rudy Dietz—A threatening, unscrupulous man. He is intent upon his own gain.

With love to Cheri Benetez,
whose special friendship is a joy and blessing in my life.

Prologue

"Are you out of your mind?" Ashley Camdon stared at her twin sister in utter disbelief.

"No, I'm just making a simple request."

"A simple request?" Ashley repeated in utter amazement.

"All you have to do is pretend to be me for just a few days until I get over this bronchitis. I've got this job that I desperately need, and I'm in no shape to start tomorrow." Jill's next fit of coughing turned into sobbing. "After all that's happened, Ashley, I just can't take any more. It's just too much…Budge leaving me the way he did and the police looking for him!"

"Honey, things always look darker when you're sick," Ashley said gently. She refrained from commenting on Jill's missing husband. This wasn't the time to point out her sister's blindness where Budge Gordon was concerned. Her marriage to the basketball star had plunged her life to an all-time low. The papers had been filled with the charges pending against her husband for illegal betting and game fixing. Budge had disappeared two months ago with thousands of dollars in betting money, leaving behind a wife and baby with bills to pay and very little income.

Ashley sighed. Jill had often mocked Ashley's view that a woman could take care of herself. But more than once she had depended upon her sister's steady presence to get her out of a jam.

"It's not as if we haven't switched places before," Jill reminded her with a wan smile. As identical twins with honey-blond hair and deep blue eyes, they had fooled teachers, friends and even boyfriends while they were growing up. But their lifestyles were now as different as those of any two siblings could be. Ashley's sedate, well-ordered life as a college professor bored Jill to death and, in turn, Ashley couldn't stand Jill's high-flying, tempestuous flare for excitement.

"But this is different," Ashley protested. "A nanny? You have to be kidding."

"This job is a godsend, Ashley. When Hugo Vandenburg offered to let me take care of his two grandkids while their parents are in Europe, I couldn't believe my luck. As owner of Budge's basketball team, he lost a lot of money because of Budge, and he sympathizes with my situation. Even though Hugo was embarrassed by a lot of negative publicity around him and the team, he was kind enough to offer me this job. If I don't show up as planned, I can kiss the job goodbye. His two grandkids are eight and ten. For heaven's sake, Ashley, you ought to be able to babysit them for a few days. And Davie's gotten used to you, so he won't be much trouble."

Ashley couldn't believe what she was hearing. She'd already flown from Denver to Atlanta to help Jill get over her illness and take care of her baby. Now her sister expected her to take the baby, go off somewhere to be a nanny to two children she'd never met and pretend that she was Mrs. Budge Gordon who had a husband running from the law.

"It's only for a few days," Jill insisted, watching Ashley's look of utter dismay. "I just couldn't show up like this, coughing my head off and looking like a rag doll that went through the washer. This nanny job will see me through the summer, and by then..." her voice trailed off, and a haunted look deepened the shadows in her face. "Maybe by then I'll have some of this sorted out."

The whole idea was crazy. Ashley couldn't believe she was even considering it. "Where does this Hugo Vandenburg live?"

"He has an estate not far from here. You can take my car, it's only a few hours drive."

"In Georgia?"

Jill nodded, but avoided looking directly at her twin. Ashley knew her sister well enough to know she was holding something back.

"Where is this place?" she asked. "Where does Hugo Vandenburg live?"

"Well, he doesn't exactly live there, I mean, not all the time. It's kind of a summer mansion," she hedged, and then took a deep breath. "His estate is on one of those small islands off the Georgia coast. You have to get to Roble Island by ferry."

Her lips trembled. "He'll hire someone else if I don't show up as planned…I mean, if you don't show up as planned."

Saying no to Jill had never been easy, and under these circumstances, a heartless refusal was almost impossible. Ashley didn't know exactly when she made the decision that she would impersonate her sister for a few days, but a harmless charade seemed the least she could do to get her sister out of a tight spot. And she *was* on summer faculty break.

"Thank you, thank you, sis," Jill kept saying gratefully between coughing spells.

"How will I know when you're ready to make the switch?" Ashley sighed in defeat.

Jill thought for a minute. "I don't want to answer the phone unless it's you. Call me every evening and leave a message on the machine…like, "Life is great." Then call me right back and I'll answer the phone. When I'm over this bug, I'll rent a car, meet you and we'll change clothes and switch cars. No one will be the wiser. Take my cell phone and use it so nobody in the house will know."

"Good idea. I brought my cell, but it only works in the Rocky Mountain area. Can you think of anything else?"

Jill shook her head, and Ashley sighed. *Oh, what a tangled web we weave when we first practice to deceive.* She'd never been any good at lies and now she was preparing to live one.

Chapter One

The ferry trip across the Sound was a short one, but long enough for Ashley's stomach to tighten with nervousness. She was supposed to call the Vandenburg house when she arrived on the ferry, and someone would come and lead the way through the marshlands and tropical woods to the estate on the Atlantic side of Roble Island.

The ferry berthed at its pier, near a main thoroughfare bordering the west side of the island. A colorful little village hugged the waterfront, tempting tourists and residents with inviting shops, restaurants, parks and several inns and motels.

She parked beside a public telephone that stood in a parking lot across from the nautically styled Seaside Inn. She dialed the number Jill had written on a slip of paper, and worried her lower lip waiting for someone to answer the insistent ring.

What if nobody was home?

A woman with a trace of an accent finally answered, "Vandenburg residence. Who is calling, please?"

"This is…Mrs. Budge Gordon." Even as she said the name for the first time, it sounded false in Ashley's ears. "I was told to call when I arrived. Someone is supposed to guide me to the house." Then she added, "I'm the new nanny."

"I'll tell Mr. Stone. Where are you?"

Ashley glanced quickly around. "I'm at the Seaside Inn," she said, and before she could ask how long it might be before her escort arrived, the woman hung up.

Great, thought Ashley. She had no idea how far away the Vandenburg house was from the wharf. Ten minutes? A half hour or more? Jill had said that the estate was on the Atlantic side of the island at its southern tip.

Davie was sleeping peacefully in his car seat, and Ashley hesitated to move him. *I should have told them I'd be waiting in the car,* she lamented. Whoever was coming for her would probably go inside the inn looking for her. Sitting in the front seat, she could watch everyone who went in and out of the white clapboard building, but the problem was that she didn't know what Mr. Stone or anyone else the woman might send looked like.

After waiting twenty minutes, she decided that she'd better unload the baby and make herself visible. Not a good start, she thought, as her natural penchant for having things well-ordered put her off balance.

She was busy unhooking the carrier from the back

seat when a red Jaguar pulled into the parking lot and parked a few stalls away. She didn't see the dark-haired slender man who got out of the car and walked toward her.

There she is, Kyle Stone thought as he took in the white Mercedes and the neat backside of the woman as she leaned over to bring a baby out of the back seat of the car and put him in a small hand carrier. Of course, she'd be driving a fancy car like that. Even though he'd never met Jill and Budge Gordon, he knew their reputation as leaders in the fast crowd of nationally known sport figures. Kyle hadn't been surprised that Budge had decided to shaft everyone and take off with illegal betting money. Keeping up their high-flying lifestyle must have been a constant financial drain.

Jill Gordon as a nanny? The idea made him hide a chuckle as he sauntered over to her car. He'd had his doubts about her ever showing up. But here she was, dressed as if she was ready for a beach party.

"Hello. You must be Mrs. Gordon," he said politely as she turned around, clumsily grasping the handle of the carrier with both hands.

Her eyes widened with surprise and obvious relief. "Are you—?"

"Kyle Stone," he answered, smiling as he quickly made a mental assessment of her. Her makeup was artfully applied to enhance her delicate features and deep liquid-blue eyes. Full lips were carefully traced with a pink, kissable lipstick, and shoulder-length, wavy, honey-blond hair framed her face. Tight jeans cupped her thighs and legs in a provocative fashion. At the moment tiny lines of a frown marred her forehead, and the skimpy summer blouse she wore didn't hide the rise and fall of her fast breathing.

"Did you have trouble finding the ferry to the island?" he asked politely. Nervousness stood out all over her.

"No, not at all." Her smile was quick and superficial. "Thank you for coming so quickly. I would like to get the baby settled at the house as soon as possible."

"Of course. It's only about a fifteen-minute drive across the island."

She wished now that she hadn't taken the baby out of his car seat. Maybe the movement of the car would lull him back to sleep. It wasn't time for another bottle, and it would be just her luck to have Davie shrieking his head off when they arrived at the house.

"I think you'll find everything you need in the nursery," Kyle said. "Mr. Vandenburg gave orders that it was to be completely equipped. What's the baby's name?" he asked politely.

"Davie."

"He's a fine fellow. So bright. Look at the way he's looking around."

Instead of smiling or responding to the compliment as he had expected a new mother would, she gave her attention to returning the baby to his car seat.

When she had trouble locking the baby in, he said, "Here, let me."

Without any argument, she stepped back and let

him do it. "I don't know why I have trouble getting that fastened," she said nervously.

Motherhood wasn't sitting well with her. Her uneasy, inept handling of the baby made him suspect that she'd turn over the baby's care to hired help the first chance she got. Any maternal instinct she had didn't show, he thought. It was a good thing that Lily McKee had been hired to help out with the kids. Jill Gordon must have been in desperate financial straits to accept Hugo's offer. Kyle certainly didn't put much faith in Mrs. Budge Gordon's ability to be any kind of a nanny.

"There you are, fellow," he said to the wide-eyed baby. Davie had golden hair fuzz and the same deep blue eyes as his mother. He wondered how any father could run off and leave his son the way Budge had.

"I guess you don't remember how to get to the house from your other visits?" Kyle said when the baby was in place and the back door closed. "Mr. Vandenburg sent his car for you on those occasions, didn't he?"

She nodded without looking at him.

"Well, just follow me. There are lots of small roads that snake through the thick stands of moss-covered oak and cypress trees. If you take the wrong one, you can wander around in a confusing maze. The Vandenburg acreage is one of the largest estates, and it's easy to get disoriented. Just stay close behind me."

Kyle walked back to his car, but before he started up the engine, he picked up his cell phone and dialed a number.

When he got his connection, he briskly told the party on the other end, ''The pigeon is in the coop. I'll keep you posted.''

THERE WAS SOMETHING ABOUT Kyle's practiced manner that put Ashley on edge. Even though he'd indicated that he hadn't met Jill, he had given her the impression that he'd been around when her twin and Budge had visited Hugo Vandenburg. She didn't like the clear assessing sharpness in his eyes, and his smile had held a subtle mocking criticism when she'd been so clumsy handling the baby carrier. She wondered what his position was at the Vandenburg estate, and hoped to heaven that she wouldn't have much contact with him.

Ashley was grateful for the red Jaguar moving ahead of her on a narrow road snaking through heavy stands of ancient live oaks hung with gray moss. Like a dark surrealistic painting, a tracery of sunlight filtered through thick branches of pine, cedar, and magnolia trees. Heavy undergrowth of myrtle bushes and palmettos masked hidden marshes and, except for the wild flight of birds disturbed by the cars' engines, Ashley couldn't see any sign of man or beast. Being used to the wide-open spaces of Colorado, she felt a tightening of claustrophobia as she drove through the dark tunnel of trees and vegetation.

Davie was growing fussy in his car seat. She knew he would be howling at the top of his lungs in a few minutes if she didn't tend to him. *That's all I need,* she thought as her hands tightened on the steering wheel.

When the landscape changed from heavy forest to low marshes bordering white beaches, she let out a grateful breath. Almost immediately, tall palmetto palms marked the entrance to a beautifully landscaped estate, and an iron gate swung open easily at Stone's light touch on his horn.

At the end of a short driveway, a southern mansion appeared almost magically in an emerald setting of trees, vines and brilliant tropical flowers. Ashley felt as if she'd just turned the pages of a fantasy book, and she had a feeling that if she just closed her eyes, the whole scene would disappear. Only the insistent, escalating cries of the baby assured her that this was no dream.

More like a nightmare, she thought as she parked behind Stone's car in front of the house and hurried to get the baby out of the back seat. She somehow managed to get him settled in the hand carrier before Kyle Stone could offer his help.

"Let me carry him," he said.

"Thanks, but I can handle him."

"Don't be silly," he chided and quickly took the carrier from her.

She wanted to protest his high-handed way of taking over because for some perverse reason she didn't want to be indebted to this self-assured, attractive man. She hated to admit that without his help, she didn't know how she would have managed her purse, diaper bag and the carrier. She had a feeling that he was deftly managing her in some fashion. Used to holding her own with the president of her college and prestigious faculty members, she chafed at being treated like an inept employee.

"I'll have Joseph bring in your luggage and the rest of the things," he assured her as she sent a questioning look at the packed car.

She managed a thank-you smile. Luckily, Davie had ceased his wailing long enough to blink his round blue eyes in the sudden sunlight, and Ashley took advantage of the moment to glance at the southern mansion.

This was a summer home? Tall white pillars graced a long veranda spanning the front of the house. Large mullioned windows dotted the first and second floors, and a pair of embossed front doors identified the entrance. Even as Ashley wondered how she would find her way around such a place, the doors flew open and two children burst out on the veranda. Stopping at the top of the stairs, they stared down at her with unsmiling, belligerent frowns.

The oldest was a ten-year-old girl, Jill had told Ashley. She had a lean girlish build and was a head taller than her sturdy eight-year-old brother. Both had dark hair, strong features and an air of superiority about them. They were staring at her with the guarded animosity of the enemy. Her teaching experience had been limited to college students who were dedicated to passing her classes. She knew nothing about appeasing youngsters who looked as if they had taken an instant dislike to her. Ashley felt her stomach take a sickening dip down into her toes.

Kyle quickly waved for the children to come down the steps. "Pamela. Benny. Meet Mrs. Gordon. This pretty lady's here to see that you have a good time this summer." He lowered the carrier so they could see the baby. "And this is Davie. I bet he's got a smile for you when he knows you better."

"Hello," Ashley said, making certain that she smiled directly at each one of them. "I'm glad to meet you." She knew Jill would have said something like, "Hi, guys, how goes it?"

Kyle tried to break the stiff moment by ruffling Benny's dark hair, winking at Pamela. "These kids are the greatest. Benny has a fantastic model airplane collection that he'd love to show you, and Pamela's going to be an Olympic swimmer, aren't you, hon? I bet Mrs. Gordon likes to swim, don't you?"

Fortunately, Ashley didn't have to lie to get in good with the little girl. Both she and Jill had been on the swim team in high school.

"I love to swim," she said quickly. "And I bet Pamela could teach me some strokes." Then she smiled at Benny. "And I would like very much to see your airplane collection."

As they walked up the steps into the house, Kyle kept up a running monologue, praising the kids and giving Pamela and Benny the impression that their new nanny was in awe of all their accomplishments.

They entered a spacious foyer decorated in white-and-black marble, and Ashley scarcely had time to view numerous doors opening off of a wide hall before Kyle whisked them up a beautiful staircase to the second floor. A spacious sitting room furnished with lounge chairs and a large television was in an open area at the top of the stairs. Ashley could tell from the childish clutter that the two children spent a lot of time there. No doubt the downstairs living rooms were off-limits.

Benny rushed over to a table, picked up a video game and held it out to Ashley. "Let's play. It's a neat airplane war game. You can have the Tomcats." Then he added with all the dictatorship of an eight-year-old, "Pammy won't play so you have to."

"She's not playing that stupid game," flared his sister. "Mother said she was supposed to keep me company in this horrid place." Her blue eyes held the hint of tears. "Grandfather had no right to make us come here."

"You're a baby…baby…baby."

"I am not." Pamela clenched her fists.

Ashley knew that if she wanted to get off on a good footing, it was important not to slight either Benny or Pamela, but at the moment she had no choice. Davie might be the smallest of the three, but his loud protests could no longer be ignored. She felt as if she were being pulled in all directions at once, and she sensed that Kyle was waiting to see what she was going to do.

"We'll play later, Benny," she promised, and caught Pamela's eyes with a reassuring smile. "I have to tend to the baby now, but there'll be time later to do the things you want.''

Neither of them responded to her promises. Both of the children were staring at her with their original belligerent frowns, and she knew that she had lost the first round by default.

"The nursery is this way," Kyle said, leading the way down the hall. Pamela and Benny didn't follow but remained in the sitting room. "I hope you'll be very comfortable here," he said as they reached the nursery, with a connecting bedroom and bath. "We want to make certain that you have a very pleasant and entertaining summer.''

Something in his tone didn't quite match the look he was giving her. She'd seen the way he'd managed the children, and she wondered if somehow he was manipulating her in the same fashion. Right then and there, she decided that she'd warn Jill about him. Ashley's intuitive sense had always stood her in good stead when dealing with people, and something about Kyle Stone did not ring true. There was a secret remoteness about him that wasn't hidden by his pleasant smile or his accommodating manner.

He set the carrier down in the nursery. "I think your little fellow's tired of traveling. I'll send Mrs. Borsch, the housekeeper, up to see if there's anything you need. She told me that she thought the nursery was pretty complete, but I'm sure you'll want everything to your own liking.''

To my own liking?

"I'm sure everything will be fine," Ashley said,

seeing diapers, a bottle warmer and other baby para-
phernalia ready and waiting. *Thank heavens, someone
had anticipated the demands of caring for a baby
twenty-four hours a day.* If she could just get through
the next few hours, things would surely smooth out.

Kyle had seen her eyes narrow as he spoke, and he
knew she'd picked up the edge of sarcasm in his tone.
Even though her reputation as the rather spoiled wife
of a notable sports figure had preceded her, he'd have
to be more careful. He didn't want to antagonize her.
If Jill Gordon got her back up, she could cause a lot
of trouble for everyone.

"Well, then, I guess I'll leave you. Mrs. Borsch
will answer any questions you have about settling in.
I'll take Pamela and Benny downstairs and keep them
busy in the library until dinnertime. I'll see you
then."

As he paused in the doorway and looked back at
her, he was struck by the awkward way she was handling the crying baby. Instead of putting the infant
over her shoulder and patting his bottom to soothe
him, she held him so that he was lying on his back,
kicking his feet and waving his arms.

He sighed inwardly. *Some nanny. It's a good thing
Pamela and Benny are old enough to manage most
things themselves.*

As he herded Benny and Pamela downstairs, his
thoughts centered on what he was going to tell Hugo
when his boss called him that night.

Nobody played Hugo Vandenburg for a fool and
got away with it. All that illegal betting money was

supposed to come home to him. All along, he'd used Budge to cover his behind-the-scenes involvement in the scam, but the basketball star had double-crossed him. Not only had Budge gotten away with Hugo's money, but he had the information that could put the wealthy team owner behind bars. The missing Budge was a loaded cannon that could go off at any minute. Hugo needed to get to him before the law did, and the whole story came out.

Thanks to a letter that Budge had written to Jill before he disappeared, Hugo was using Jill as bait to get Hugo. In the letter, Budge had declared his love for his wife and promised not to leave the country without her. Budge had given the letter to one of his player friends to deliver to Jill, but the friend had betrayed him and given the letter to Hugo instead.

Hugo had offered the deserted Jill Gordon a nanny's job in order to have her under surveillance. He'd put Kyle in charge of keeping close tabs on her. Kyle's orders were to carefully monitor any contact that Budge might make with his wife so that any plans the couple made to leave the country together could be foiled.

But relating to Jill Gordon was going to be a harder job than Kyle had thought. She was less than competent caring for her own baby and having her handling two more children was likely to result in a fiasco. Unfortunately, there was too much at stake to let her sink or swim on her own. Hugo had really hoodwinked her into thinking that he considered her another one of Budge's victims and wanted to make it up to her out of the goodness of his heart.

Chapter Two

After she'd diapered Davie and heated the last bottle of formula, Ashley collapsed in a rocking chair with the baby in her arms. Fighting his little fists away from his mouth so she could stick in the bottle, she soothed him and breathed a sigh of relief when he finally recognized the rubber nipple. At first he almost choked on the flow of the warm liquid, but after a moment, he settled into a quiet nursing rhythm.

As she sat there in the quiet room, the silence broken only by Davie's contented slurping, some of the stiffness went out of her body. She leaned her head back against the chair. *I can do this. It's only for a few days.* Jill had always been able to take life at a gallop. She'd probably thrive on all the commotion and excitement of living in a grand southern mansion.

The baby was almost finished with his bottle when Ashley realized someone was standing in the doorway watching her.

"May I come in?" the woman asked briskly.

Ashley nodded. "Please, do."

"Mr. Stone told me you had arrived, Mrs. Gordon. I'm Ina Borsch, the housekeeper." Her unsmiling eyes flickered over Ashley and the baby.

"Nice to meet you, Mrs. Borsch," Ashley said politely to the large-boned woman, obviously stiffly corseted under a plain navy blue dress. She recognized her voice; this was the woman who had answered the telephone.

"I trust you have found everything to your satisfaction. Mr. Vandenburg left instructions that you were to be made comfortable. I have done my best to carry out his orders."

"Thank you for your concern, Mrs. Borsch," Ashley responded in the same formal tone. The woman's manner indicated that she didn't share the same concern about Ashley's comfort. It was hard to judge the housekeeper's age—fiftyish, Ashley guessed. Her broad face held an expression of disapproval that reminded Ashley of a general looking over new recruits and finding them wanting. One thing was clear. Ina Borsch expected everyone to acknowledge her position and authority as housekeeper and behave accordingly.

It wasn't Ashley's nature to knuckle under anyone, but the whole situation had put her off-balance. At the moment, she had little choice but to play the role that Jill had forced on her.

Mrs. Borsch glanced around the nursery. "I think you'll find all the supplies you need. Even though it's been some time since we had a baby in the house, I made sure that all the necessities are here."

"Yes, I found the diapers and bottle warmer." Ashley told her, hoping she sounded more motherly than she felt. "I'll be needing to sterilize some bottles for Davie and make some more formula for his next feeding."

"Lily will see to those needs," the housekeeper said with a dismissing wave of her large hand.

"Lily?"

"One of the housemaids. Mr. Vandenburg has left instructions that Lily is to be assigned to the nursery while you are here."

Once again, Ashley could tell from the woman's tone that this decision wasn't hers. Obviously the welcome mat wasn't out for Jill Gordon as far as Ina Borsch was concerned. Was it a personal prejudice, or was there something deeper at the root of her simmering hostility? Ashley decided to play the innocent and see what she could find out about the household from this martinet housekeeper.

"Mr. Vandenburg is such a nice man," Ashley said in her sister's bubbly tone. "He's always been so good to Budge and me. I just know I'm going to love being here. Benny and Pamela are such darlings. And that nice Mr. Stone, meeting me the way he did and all. Is he related to Hugo, too?" Her chatter sounded so false in her own ears that Ashley was secretly embarrassed by it.

"No, Kyle Stone is an employee like the rest of us. Mr. Vandenburg leaves him in charge when he's away on business." Then her heavy chin lifted. "The house and staff are my responsibility, and I handle them as I see fit.''

''It can't be easy,'' Ashley said, sinking so low as to try and soften her up by the use of flattery. ''You must have an awfully big staff to run this house.''

''Only when Mr. Vandenburg is in residence, then the staff is doubled. When he's away, there are two maids, a cook, my husband, Joseph, and Mr. Stone…and now you,'' she added. Once again, her disapproval was obvious. ''This is the first time the grandchildren have required a nanny. Usually they travel in the summer with their parents.''

Ashley remembered Pamela's remark that it was their grandfather's fault that they were spending the summer here. ''Then the children are not used to a nanny?''

''Not at their grandfather's house. You're the first.'' And her tone inferred that she hoped she would be the last.

''Have you been here a long time, Mrs. Borsch?'' Ashley prodded. She wanted to relay all the information she could to Jill, so her twin wouldn't have to start from square one learning about the staff.

Surprisingly enough, Ina Borsch seemed willing to talk about herself. ''Up until five years ago we were in Mr. Vandenburg's Atlanta household. When his wife died, he bought this place. My husband enjoys the island more than I do,'' she said flatly. ''Joseph is the groundskeeper and helps me in the house when there are extra duties. He'll be bringing up your luggage. And as soon as Lily finishes her chores in the kitchen, she can tend to your needs." Her tone made it clear that a nanny's presence in the house caused everyone more work. "You will be responsible for making your own bed daily and for keeping your room and the nursery in presentable order. Once a week, one of the maids will clean."

Ashley nodded. Keeping the nursery, bedroom and bath in presentable condition wouldn't be any hardship. She wasn't used to hired help, but she didn't know about Jill. Housekeeping wasn't one of her twin's strong suits.

Apparently, Mrs. Borsch had decided that she'd wasted enough time in chitchat. She took a sheet of folded paper from her pocket and placed it on a small table near the rocking chair where Ashley was rocking the baby. "Mr. Vandenburg left this for you. It's a daily schedule for the children. You are to spend from nine until twelve every morning in the library with them, supervising organized activities such as reading, art and music. They have all the materials they need, and he assumed that you would be able to manage such educational supervision."

"I believe I can handle it," Ashley said, smothering a smile. She was quite practiced in lecturing a theater of college students on those subjects. She was certain she could manage the studies of an eight- and a ten-year-old.

"Mr. Vandenburg has requested that you spend two to three hours in the afternoon on outside activities. These could include swimming, hiking, outdoor games, beach walking and any other activities that seem appropriate.''

Ashley nodded. The schedule seemed deceptively easy, and mingled with a sense of relief was a suspicion that the formidable housekeeper was holding something back.

"During your morning and afternoon activities, Lily will tend the baby and also, during the lunch and dinner hours. You will eat in the small dining room with Mr. Stone when he's present, and alone when he's away from the house.''

"And the evenings?''

"The children will amuse themselves with television, games or other chosen activities. Lily will make certain that lights are out by eight-thirty. Are there any questions?''

Mrs. Borsch's authoritative manner did not invite any discussion, and Ashley wondered how soon it would be before the two children rebelled against such a regimented routine. If Pamela and Benny had never stayed here without their parents, she doubted that this rigid daily structure was one they were used to.

"The schedule seems workable,'' Ashley lied.

Mrs. Borsch surveyed the contented baby in Ashley's arms, and for a moment Ashley thought she might say something soft and gentle, but instead she frowned. "I hope you can keep him quiet during the night. None of us want to lose our sleep listening to a crying baby.''

"I'll do my best, but he's had a touch of colic that makes him fretful at night."

Without commenting, the housekeeper turned toward the door, and Ashley watched her broad straight back disappear into the hall. No welcome mat, for sure, on Mrs. Borsch's part. Maybe Jill would be able to thaw the housekeeper out, Ashley thought, feeling as if she'd just flunked some kind of test.

Ashley had the baby over her shoulder, burping him when a tall, angular, gray-haired man appeared in the doorway of the nursery.

"Where do you want the bags?" His weathered face, shadowed eyes and lean cheeks lacked any hint of a smile. If anything, Joseph Borsch was more reticent than his wife.

"In the bedroom, please." She could sort out the baby's things later and put them away in the chest of drawers under the diapering table. "Thank you."

He just nodded, left the luggage and then disappeared without any indication that she was any more than a chore to be finished with as soon as possible.

Carefully getting to her feet, Ashley put the sleeping baby down in the crib that had been made up with pretty bedding. Davie looked perfectly happy and contented in his new surroundings, which was more than she could say for herself. She'd never felt more out of place in her life.

When she went into the adjoining bedroom to unpack, Jill's leather luggage looked totally unfamiliar sitting in the middle of a beautiful Asian rug. Just as the purse she'd been carrying with all of Jill's identification felt foreign to her, Ashley had trouble identifying with the matching suitcases and cosmetic bag bearing her sister's name.

As she hung up Jill's wardrobe, the charade she was playing suddenly hit home. The whole idea of trying to live her sister's life for her, even for a few days, demanded a kind of deceit that went against every grain in her body. She had always prided herself on her integrity, and something about the house and the people in it warned her that they would not take any hint of deceit lightly. She shivered as a bone-deep chill went through her.

"I could have hung those clothes up for you."

Ashley swung around, startled to see a young woman standing only a couple of feet behind her, watching.

"Sorry if I frightened you, Mrs. Gordon. I'm Lily, ma'am." She gave Ashley a wide, broad smile that crinkled the corners of her brown eyes. Carrot-red hair lay in a thick braid around Lily's full face, and a scattering of freckles marched across her nose. Her white blouse and blue skirt were rather rumpled, and she nervously smoothed the folds over her ample hips. Ashley doubted if she was more than eighteen or nineteen. Her open friendliness was a surprise.

"Nice to meet you, Lily. I'm Jill." Using her sister's name didn't come easily, but Ashley knew that she'd have to get used to answering to it during the next few days. "I have a feeling you're going to be a godsend."

"Hope so, ma'am." Lily's tentative smile broadened as she reached for the hanger that Ashley had in her hands, and deftly hung it beside the other clothes. As Lily's eyes passed over the riot of colors and fancy fabrics, she murmured appreciatively, "You sure have pretty clothes."

Ashley smothered a smile. A good sign. Jill and Lily would get along fine. Suddenly, she felt much better about the whole situation.

Ashley asked Lily about sterilizing the baby's bottles and making more formula, and she was relieved at the easy but efficient way Lily worked to do everything Ashley asked her. They put the baby's things away, and when Davie woke up, Lily cooed over him and deftly began to change his diaper.

Watching out of the corner of her eye, Jill was relieved to see how confidently Lily handled the infant. Not only did she seem perfectly at ease, but she seemed to enjoy herself as she chattered to Davie, telling him what a fine fellow he was, and trying to coax a smile.

"You're very good with him, Lily," Ashley said, wondering if she had babies of her own even though there was no sign of a wedding ring.

"My mother had eight children and I'm the oldest. There are four still at home." Then she added, "We moved to the island a year ago from the mainland. My Da is a fisherman, and he thought he could bring in a better catch living here." She sighed. "I sure need to keep this job."

"I'm sure you will. A big place like this must need lots of help."

She frowned. "There aren't many people around for such a big place. Most of the house is shut off. It's a funny thing, though. Even when there are people in the guest cottage, it's off-limits to the house staff. I guess they bring their own help. Right now only Mr. Stone is living there, but none of us are allowed to go there to clean or anything." She looked puzzled. "Sometimes I hear people coming and going in the night. Once I asked Mr. Stone about it, and he just laughed and told me not to worry my pretty head about it." A hint of color rose in her cheeks. "He teases me sometimes, and Mrs. Borsch gets mad when he pays me any attention. I think he's a really nice guy, don't you?"

"He seems pleasant enough," Ashley conceded, but she wasn't about to give him a rave review. She had the feeling he was adept at manipulating everyone, including Lily. Having her meals with Kyle Stone could turn out to be a tense affair. She'd have to watch everything she said.

ASHLEY WENT DOWNSTAIRS a few minutes before eight o'clock, following the directions that Lily had given her. "Go down the main hall, past the solarium, and turn right. There's a small family dining room that overlooks the back garden and stone patio. A lovely spot, it is," Lily assured. "The large dining room isn't used unless Mr. Vandenburg is here with guests."

She had changed her mind several times about what to wear; had been tempted to wear slacks and a summer top, but she didn't want to embarrass herself if dressing up for dinner was expected. There was no doubt in Ashley's mind that her sister would delight in wearing some of her nice dresses in the evening, so she'd chosen a bright red sheath with a short, tight skirt and spaghetti straps—the simplest and most colorful of all her sister's dresses.

Even though dangling earrings were anathema to Ashley, Jill wore jewelry with everything, so she had put on a silver pair that swung easily with the turn of her head. In some ways she felt as if she were dressed for a costume party, but the excitement churning her stomach was not from joy.

Maybe Kyle Stone won't be here for dinner. Maybe I'll have a nice quiet dinner by myself, and I won't have to face his inquisitive eyes.

Hope was born as she reached the small dining room, and paused for a moment in the doorway. The room was beautifully furnished in ivory and burgundy. A crystal chandelier with loops of roped glass glittered over a round table, and gold-tinted ivory chairs with burgundy velvet seats flanked the table. A mirrored buffet facing the door reflected an unfamiliar Ashley, standing there with apprehension in her rounded eyes.

When the slender man wearing a white coat and dark trousers turned around from a small bar at the end of the room, she knew her hopes were only wishful thinking.

"Good evening, Mrs. Gordon. You look lovely tonight."

Chapter Three

Kyle had been betting with himself that Jill Gordon would show up for dinner in some sexy outfit, but he wasn't prepared for the sudden start he experienced when he saw her in the doorway. Her honey-blond hair was swept up in a casual twist, and silver earrings glittering like moving stars framed her lovely face. As she came toward him, the soft material of her red dress rippled over long silk stockings and clung to her waist and breasts.

"Lovely," he repeated, and tightened the hold on his glass as he greeted her. She was one sexy female.

"Thank you. I wasn't certain whether or not I should dress for dinner, but I see that I made the right choice," she said as she let her eyes travel over his jacket, pleated white shirt and gold cuff links. Dark eyebrows accented his dark brown eyes and a generous mouth was nicely framed with a dimpled chin and firm cheeks. He was what Jill would have called "drop-dead handsome."

"I couldn't pass up the opportunity to make this

an occasion," he answered smoothly. "Your first night here should be treated as something special. Putting our best foot forward, so to speak."

"Do you do that for all the new help?"

He mentally stiffened. There was a depth to her eyes that was disconcerting. The usual bland flattery wasn't working the way he expected. Above everything else, he didn't want to alert her to the fact that her presence here was anything beyond her duties as a nanny.

"Hugo gave instructions to make you welcome," he said smoothly. "May I offer you a drink? I don't want to brag but my skills as a bartender are equal to any challenge."

For some perverse reason, Ashley remembered a popular drink the college students had touted for a while. Before she had time to think about it, she said, "How about Sex on the Beach?"

He was tempted to ask if that was an offer, but he restrained himself. This was the good-time, party girl that he'd been expecting. In a way, he was relieved. Keeping Jill Gordon happy might be easier than he thought.

He set down his Scotch and soda. "Sex on the Beach coming up. I'll make you the best one you ever had."

That won't be hard, since I've never had one, thought Ashley, already put-out with herself for not asking for her usual daiquiri. Now she had one more thing she'd have to warn her twin about when they switched places. Asking Jill what she was drinking nowadays had never occurred to her. It would be just like Jill to say, "I never drink anything but martinis."

"Here you go." Kyle handed her a bubbling pink drink, and waited for her to take a sip.

"Mmmm," Ashley murmured, hoping she was making the right response. The drink had a pleasant punch flavor, but she worried about how much of a kick was hidden in its sweetness.

He picked up the small pitcher that contained the remainder of her drink, and set it on the dining table where two places had been set facing each other. "Gerta will be serving in a few minutes. She knows I like to enjoy a drink before dinner. Please sit down, Jill. May I call you, Jill?" he asked as he guided in her chair.

"Yes, of course," she said, trying to quell a nervous tightening in her stomach. How in the world could she avoid the dangerous pitfalls inherent in any idle dinner conversation when the truth must be laced with lies?

"First names seem better all around even though Hugo frowns on too much familiarity amongst the staff," he said. "We all toe the mark when he's around, but you know the old adage—when the cat's away." He took the chair opposite her. "I'm delighted to have such a vivacious dinner partner. Since we'll be seeing a lot of each other, we might as well get better acquainted."

Ashley tried to keep a pleasant smile on her face as she fought off a rising sense of panic. Now what? He obviously expected some entertaining table conversation. What if he started asking her questions whose answers he already knew?

Deciding offense was her own defense, she asked, "Where'd you learn to tend bar?"

Kyle set down his drink slowly. The question took him by surprise because he'd expected the conversation to totally revolve around Jill Gordon. From what he'd heard, this gal pretty much commanded the center of attention wherever she went. "A pretty dull story," he parried. "Not the kind to interest a pretty lady."

"Try me," she challenged, steadily meeting his eyes over the rim of her glass.

"All right." He leaned back in the chair. "My father had a small tavern in a New York Irish ghetto, where I grew up. We lived in a flat above the bar, and I guess I was more at home working with my pa than upstairs with my five sisters and my mother. What about you? Where'd you learn to appreciate Sex on the Beach—the drink, I mean?" he added with a flirtatious grin.

"I've been to a few parties," Ashley said lightly, resenting his suggestive tone. Jill's personal life was none of Kyle Stone's business. He was, after all, just an employee of Hugo Vandenburg, as she was. The way he'd deftly turned the conversation back onto her made it difficult to keep the questions going in his direction. She sensed that there was a war of sorts going on between them.

"What about your family?" he prodded.

She stalled, lifting her glass to her lips again, and

suddenly realized that her drink was nearly gone. Never in her life had she drunk a cocktail so fast.

"Here, let me fill that up," Kyle said as he saw her looking at her glass. *She was a drinker, all right,* he thought as he took the pitcher and filled her glass again. She had downed her drink in record time. His orders were to make sure that her stay as nanny was a successful one, even if he had to pick up the slack with the children. Keeping her on the job was going to be one heck of a challenge if she were a lush. Just his luck that he'd have to put an inebriated Jill Gordon to bed her first night here. Where was Gerta with the food?

As Ashley watched him fill her glass again, she realized that in her nervousness she'd consumed the first drink much too fast. The clear thoughts she needed so desperately in order to get through this dinner without a catastrophe were already becoming fuzzy. Her sister would never forgive her if she fouled up everything the first night here. *I have to keep the talk general and away from any personal revelations,* she told herself. She already had the feeling that Kyle knew enough about Jill to make any conversation a minefield.

As she let her gaze wander around the room, searching for some neutral topic, she murmured, "Very nice decor."

"Hugo renovated the whole house last winter," Kyle said, glancing at his watch.

Ashley pretended interest in the ivory-and-burgundy floral wallpaper and framed prints of southern colonial life hung in an artistic grouping above the mirrored buffet. As her gaze moved to a corner of the room, she suddenly stiffened, blinked and stared. Were her eyes deceiving her?

"What's the matter?" he asked, seeing her startled expression.

"That freestanding corner cabinet..."

He followed her gaze. "Yes. What's the matter with it?"

"It looks in perfect condition," she answered without thinking as her eyes swept over the dark walnut wood. The only time she'd seen one like it was in the textbook she used to teach about life in the colonial period. The cabinet's fluted pilasters and classical moldings revealed the close relationship between cabinetwork and architecture that was observed in the colonies as early as 1715. There was no doubt in Ashley's mind that this was a museum piece. She opened her mouth to share this wonderful discovery and then realized from the look on his face that she'd stepped into quicksand. "My aunt had one like that," she lied.

"Are you interested in antique furniture, Jill?" he asked with a rather mocking smile. "Mr. Vandenburg has a hobby of buying up old estates, you know."

"No, I didn't," she answered truthfully. This was a surprise. From what Jill had said, Ashley hadn't expected the wealthy man to be a collector.

"You'll probably find quite a few pieces in the house, as well as old china and porcelain," he said casually.

"Nice hobby," she answered in what she hoped

was a matter-of-fact tone that would hide her excitement. No telling what treasures the man had picked up if this lovely walnut cupboard was any indication of his tastes, she thought. Her historical studies had created an insatiable passion for beautiful antiques. Maybe she'd have a chance to see some of them before she and Jill switched places. Thinking about her twin brought Ashley up short. She knew it would be out of character for Jill to be interested in "old things." In fact, she knew what her sister's response to all of this would be.

"I bet they're worth a lot of money," Ashley said.

Kyle smiled. *Money.* For a few minutes there, her interest in the old cupboard had thrown him an unexpected curve. The pretty lady's interest in an old cupboard didn't fit in with the profile that he'd been given. Now, he knew her interest was centered on cold, hard cash.

"I guess there's a market for that stuff," he agreed, deciding he'd have to make sure that they kept temptation out of her way. Money was money, and he didn't want her lifting any gold snuff boxes or rare coins. He knew she was financially stressed, and he'd seen the light of interest in her eyes when he told her about Hugo's penchant for antiques. Yes, indeed, this gal was going to require a lot more attention than he'd been led to believe. Hugo would have his neck for sure if something happened to even one of his prize acquisitions.

At that moment Gerta came in with the dinner trays. The maid looked harried, and Kyle wondered if her uncle, the cook, had been at her again. Hugo had brought a distant relative of his, Hendrick Heinz, from Germany to cook for him, and Gerta, the cook's niece, had come along, too. She was a very plain woman in her thirties, and Kyle had decided that she had a personality as colorless as her looks. The only time Gerta showed any animation was when she was fighting with her uncle, and the kitchen rocked as they spewed a volley of German curses at each other. Kyle had learned to give them a wide berth, leaving Mrs. Borsch to deal with the volatile pair. The only saving grace were the wonderful meals that the bombastic Hendrick prepared.

"Thank you, Gerta," Kyle said, as she began to place covered dishes on the table. Then he smiled at Ashley, "You're in for a treat. I'll guarantee that you've never tasted better cooking anywhere. The menu is always varied, even when Hugo is gone. I hope you're not watching that slim figure of yours so much you don't enjoy good food."

As his eyes lingered a moment on her tight-fitting dress, Ashley felt a spurt of irritation. Why did she have the feeling he was constantly baiting her?

"Oh, is that a problem for you?" she answered, looking at him with what she hoped was wide-eyed innocence. "Luckily, I'm able to eat whatever I want without worrying. I suppose some people have problems with over-eating."

As Gerta placed a steaming bowl of lobster bisque in front of her, Ashley smiled at the maid, but she kept her head lowered and avoided any eye contact as she moved around the table.

"Wine?" Kyle offered as he took an iced bottle out of a wine bucket and reached for her goblet.

"No, thank you," Ashley said quickly. She was still feeling the effects of her first drink, and was determined to keep her mind clear for the match of wits they were playing. "I'd prefer a cup of coffee with dinner," she said.

"Yes, of course," Kyle said, surprised. "Coffee for the lady, Gerta." He saw then that she hadn't touched her second drink.

Dinner wasn't going at all the way he had imagined. He'd been prepared for a light flirtation on her part, accompanied by a lot of superficial chitchat. He was getting all kinds of mixed vibes from her. A deep uneasiness began to gnaw at him. What if she wasn't the fluffy-headed yuppie that he'd been led to believe? That could complicate matters with frightening consequences. Maybe Jill Gordon had a hidden agenda of her own in coming here?

"Delicious soup," Ashley murmured, and when the main course of medaillons of veal with creamed asparagus and sautéed sugar snap peas was served, she didn't have to pretend to enjoy the delicious meal.

Her dinner partner had fallen strangely silent, and Ashley began to relax. She didn't know how she was going to manage it, but she wasn't going to put herself through this every evening. Using the baby or the children as an excuse, she'd keep her distance from Mr. Stone and make some other arrangement for dinner. Jill could handle the situation any way she wanted, but Ashley wasn't up to any more games of cat-and-mouse.

When they had finished a mouthwatering cappuccino truffle for dessert, Ashley wiped her mouth with the linen napkin and said, "You were right. The dinner was wonderful. I'd like to thank the cook personally."

"No," Kyle said, quickly rising to his feet before she did. "Not a good idea. I mean, Hendrick is rather temperamental. Almost everyone in the house views his kitchen as enemy territory. I give him a wide berth. Just tell Mrs. Borsch and she'll pass along the compliment."

Ashley frowned. "It sounds as if you're not one of his favorite people."

"Let's say I've lost a few skirmishes." He came around the table and slipped her chair back. "I'll see you upstairs."

As she stood up, his warm breath touched her neck and a teasing scent of a spicy cologne teased her nostrils. His nearness was unsettling, and she wished that he'd forget about being the polite host and let her go back to her room by herself—if she could find it.

As they started down the long main hall past several closed doors, Ashley asked, "Which room is the library? I thought I'd take a quick look around and see what I might use with Pamela and Benny tomorrow. According to the schedule Mrs. Borsch gave me, I have to keep them busy in the library until noon."

"It's right off the music room," he said as he

stopped in front of a set of double doors. He opened them, reached inside and flipped on a light to reveal a high ceiling and floor-to-ceiling bookcases lining the walls.

Ashley's eyes widened as they entered the spacious room. It was filled with myriad books and tastefully furnished with small reading tables, comfortable chairs and brown leather couches. A modern computer stood on a desk in one corner.

"You look surprised," Kyle said with an edge of amusement at Ashley's obvious stunned reaction.

"I have to confess that I didn't expect such a complete library," she admitted.

Was the room just for show, or did Hugo Vandenburg have as much interest in reading as he did in sports? Somehow Ashley hadn't pictured the wealthy game owner as an intellectual. Jill had given her the impression that Vandenburg was a hard-nosed businessman who had little interest in anything but a winning team, and a good return on his investment.

Kyle walked over to a library table where some books and boxes were stacked. "Here are some schoolbooks and supplies which Pamela and Benny's mother left for them. She was concerned that they were missing their usual summer educational program, and she wasn't happy about them spending the summer here."

"The children don't seem very happy about it, either," Ashley commented, thoughtfully. "I wonder why the decision was made to leave them here?"

Kyle didn't like the way the conversation was go-

ing. This kind of questioning could backfire if he gave
the wrong answers. "It was their grandfather's idea,"
he offered with a slight shrug. "I guess he wanted to
spend more time with them."

"But does he? I mean, does he spend more time
with them when they're here?"

"When he can," Kyle answered vaguely. "I imagine Hugo will want a report from you from time to
time about the children's studies," he said, deliberately stretching the truth. Hugo had told him not to
worry about anything but keeping her and the kids
occupied, but Kyle suddenly decided it might be better if she concentrated on their studies rather than asking questions that might prove dangerous to everyone.
"Benny and Pamela can probably tell you what subjects their mother wants them to study."

As she fingered through the schoolbooks, he studied her expression, but he couldn't tell how she was
reacting to the challenge of teaching. He wouldn't be
surprised if neither of the kids opened a book while
they were holed up in the library for two hours every
day. The schedule was one that the children's mother
had insisted upon. Hugo hadn't cared one way or the
other, but had agreed in order to get his way.

"The music room is there," he said, pointing to an
archway at the far end of the library. "Would you
like to see it?"

She nodded. "Yes, please."

As he turned on the lights, he decided that it was
a good bet that Jill Gordon and the kids would spend

more time in the music room listening to CDs than in the library, reading.

Once again, Ashley was startled by the elegance of the house and its furnishings. In the music room, mirrored walls and murals provided a plush backdrop for a grand piano, an entertainment center and various musical instruments, complete with stands and music.

When Kyle saw her questioning eyes lingering on the assortment of instruments, he explained, "Hugo likes his guests to have everything they need to perform and entertain,"

"And do you perform and entertain, also?" Ashley asked.

Kyle tensed because he knew that there was more to her question than appeared on the surface. Her swiftness and perception were completely unexpected. Had she intuitively picked up his aversion to being Vandenburg's puppet? "I'm afraid I'm a little short on the entertainment side," he said evasively. "How about you? Didn't Hugo tell me that you played the guitar for his guests when you and your husband visited?"

Jill hadn't told her that little happening. What else had her sister left out? Ashley pretended she was too interested in the room to answer.

"How about a little after-dinner music?" He picked up one of the guitars and handed it to her.

The way he was looking at her made her wonder if he was testing her or just being spontaneous. In any case, he'd backed her into a corner. Even though both she and Jill had taken guitar lessons, Jill was the one

who had played in a band after high-school gradua-
tion, while Ashley had barely mastered a few chords.

"Your reputation precedes you," he warned her
with a smile.

She forced a laugh. "I'll tell you what. Let me do
a little practicing, and maybe by next week I'll show
off a little bit."

"Fair enough," he said. "I'll look forward to it."

I'll have to warn Jill, she thought as they went back
into the library. The list of things she needed to coach
her twin about was getting longer and longer.

Kyle watched Ashley's mouth tighten as she picked
up a couple of the textbooks to take with her. She
was worried. He could tell. What if she backed out
of the nanny job because she couldn't cut the mustard
as a teacher?

He immediately shifted into damage-control mode
and said, "I wouldn't worry too much about any formal lessons. Just keep Benny and Pamela occupied
as best you can. It *is* summer, after all."

She wanted to remind him about his earlier warn-
ings. And now he was giving her mixed signals about
what was expected of her as a nanny? How much
weight did he have when it came to Hugo's decisions? She was confused as to his role in the household, but one thing was sure, she couldn't afford to
risk him knowing that Jill was pulling a fast one on
him.

As he shut the library doors, he asked, "Would you
like to see the solarium?"

Without waiting for her answer, he took her arm

and guided her through an arched doorway into a dimly lit room filled with beautiful plants, exquisite flowers and tropical greenery. Moonlight and stars shone through a domed glass ceiling, and small lights scattered through the flowers beds twinkled like stars and gave a soft illumination to the room. The air was redolent with heady perfume, and the only sound was a soft musical waterfall flowing over rocks into a small pond that glistened in the moonlight.

The room was designed so perfectly that the lush garden outside blended harmoniously with the plants on the inside. It was difficult to tell where one started and the other began. Ashley's senses were assaulted by the sensuous beauty around her. She was grateful for Kyle's silence as she touched the delicate petals of a white orchid, and lifted her eyes to the high canopy of sky and stars overhead. Surrounded by beautiful flowering plants of every kind, she truly felt as if she'd suddenly entered some kind of fairyland.

When she turned to smile at him, she forgot about any pretense. "Thank you for sharing this with me."

Her reaction was not at all what Kyle had expected. He'd only offered to show her the solarium out of politeness, in order that she would know which rooms she could use and which ones were off-limits.

"It's so beautiful, it's almost unreal, isn't it?"

He searched her face and found only sincerity in her shining eyes. The glow on her face was more seductive than her dangling earrings or the tantalizing rise and fall of her full breasts. A surge of sexual warmth took him off guard. He knew he'd better squelch it—and quickly!

"Is it all right if I come here often?" she asked, hopefully.

"The only one who might object is Joseph. He's possessive about his plants, inside and out," he said shortly, angry with her for having gotten to him with her shining eyes and awed expression. "But I'm sure you can win him over. I can't imagine any man resisting your charms for long."

He knew his snide remark had hit its target when her eyes lost their shine as she turned away from him. Just as well, he thought. He had to keep his priorities straight. There was too much at stake for him to jeopardize months of careful effort because she knew how to send a man's hormones into orbit.

She fell silent as they walked down the hall. "I'll see you to your room," he said when they reached the main staircase to the floors above.

"There's no need. I know my way from here. Good night and thanks for showing me around."

Ashley quickly brushed past him and was halfway up the stairs when she realized that he was mounting the stairs behind her. She swung around to face him, ready to dismiss him with her professional hauteur. "Why are you following me?"

His mouth tightened. "Even though the tantalizing allure of you climbing the stairs in that tight dress is worth viewing, Jill, I assure you that my intention is not to follow you. We just happen to be going in the same direction."

"But I thought you were staying in the guest house."

Kyle raised an eyebrow. Someone had been talking to her about him. Probably Lily. Sometimes that gal knew more than was good for her. He wondered what else Jill Gordon had picked up on the household grapevine.

"Yes, I'm in the guest house, but I've been looking in on the kids every night. And if they're not asleep, I talk to them a little while." He gave her that sardonic smile of his. "I hope that's all right with their new nanny?"

Ashley didn't even grace his remark with an answer. She turned on her heel, and climbed the rest of the stairs without looking back. Fuming silently, she went down the hall to the nursery and closed the door behind her with a punctuating bang that startled Lily.

What was worse, it woke up the baby!

Whatever she'd said about enjoying the solarium was obviously not to his liking, but then why show it to her in the first place? She was bewildered by the sudden distance he'd put between them. What had she done wrong?

Chapter Four

Lily went quickly over to the crib, turned Davie on his stomach and began patting his little rear. "There, there, back to sleep, now. Back to sleep," she soothed until his cries had faded away and he was sound asleep again.

"I'm sorry," Ashley apologized quietly, embarrassed that her irritation with Kyle had gotten the best of her. "Thanks for getting him back to sleep. I wasn't thinking when I closed the door so hard."

Lily looked at her with raised eyebrows. "You in a snit about something? Didn't you enjoy your dinner?"

"Dinner was fine," Ashley answered evenly. She didn't want to discuss the evening's happenings. Her emotions were in some kind of a tangle, and she needed time to sort everything out.

Lily followed her into the bedroom. "Was Mr. Stone there?" she asked. At Ashley's nod, she sighed. "Isn't he something?"

He was "something," all right, Ashley silently

agreed. She'd never had a man create such a yo-yo of emotions within her. Her usual calm, confident interaction with other people had deserted her. The whole evening had been like a jousting contest, and she was worn-out.

"Does he check on Pamela and Benny every night?" Ashley asked, disgusted with herself for bothering to validate his story. What did it matter? She planned to give him a wide berth from now on.

"Well, I usually get the children settled in bed by nine, but I know that they don't go right to sleep because in the morning there are books and stuff all over their beds. Benny said something about Mr. Stone reading to him."

So he wasn't lying. For some reason that surprised Ashley, and she began to feel foolish about accusing him of following her.

Lily sighed. "He's such a nice man. I just can't believe all the things they say about him."

"What things?" Ashley's interest was immediate. Even though gossiping with this young maid wasn't the kind of behavior that she admired, she was going to do it just the same.

Lily's expression suddenly became guarded. "Sometimes my tongue gets the better of me. It's none of my business what goes on around here. Mr. Stone has always been fair with me, and I'm not a bit afraid of him."

"Afraid of him? Is there some reason you should be?"

Lily's eyes rounded "I wouldn't be asking things

like that if I were you, Jill," she warned. "And, please, don't be saying I was talking out of turn. If you start asking questions, I'm likely to get my walking papers. Promise?"

"Of course, Lily." Ashley assured her. No doubt the truth about Kyle would probably surface from other sources if she kept her ears open. Her own intuitive sense of his duplicity seemed to be validated by what Lily was afraid to tell her. Finding out as much as she could about him before Jill took over suddenly took on major importance.

"Thanks for looking after the baby, Lily. Now, I'd better get to bed and get some sleep before Davie wakes up for his night feeding."

"There are three bottles of formula left," Lily said. "That should carry him until I can make up some more in the morning."

"You're an angel, Lily. I don't think I could manage without you," she said with more truth than the maid would ever know.

"Davie's a dear. It's a dirty shame the way your husband up and left you penniless with a raft of debts. Some of them are saying that you've got money stashed away, but I don't believe it. Why would you take on a nanny's job if you didn't have to?"

Ashley blinked. The gossip mill had done its work on Jill, all right. No telling what stories were going around about Budge and the missing money. As if her sister were talking through her, Ashley said, "I need this job. And I intend to do my best to keep it."

"Oh, I don't think you have to worry. I heard Mrs.

Borsch say that Mr. Vandenburg had given it to you out of the kindness of his heart, that all he really wanted was a babysitter for the summer… not a real nanny.''

"Really?" Ashley frowned. Something didn't add up. "Mrs. Borsch made it clear what the daily schedule is to be, and what I am supposed to accomplish during those hours. She certainly didn't give me the impression that I was to be a glorified babysitter and neither did Kyle Stone."

Lily shrugged and started toward the door. "I guess you'll find out soon enough."

"What time do the children have breakfast?"

"Between eight and eight-thirty, usually on the garden terrace, but I heard Mr. Stone tell Gerta that he would be having breakfast with you in the dining room." She frowned. "That's kinda strange. He usually has Gerta bring a tray to the guest house in the mornings." Then her mouth eased into a smile. "I guess he was just waiting for a pretty lady to join him." She winked at Ashley and disappeared into the hall.

Glancing at her watch, Ashley saw that it was nine-thirty. She'd promised to call Jill at bedtime every night to let her know that everything was under control. *Was everything under control?* Ashley asked herself as she closed the hall door and took Jill's cell phone from her purse.

She dialed Jill's number, and when the answering machine came on, she left the coded message, "Life is great.'' Then hung up. When she dialed a second time, her twin picked it up on the second ring.

"Ashley?"

"Yes, it's me. How are you doing?"

Ashley's heart sank when Jill had a bout of coughing before answering. She knew that her twin wasn't any better than she had been when she'd left her that morning. Ashley's hand tightened on the phone.

Jill croaked, "The doctor is changing my prescription, and he says I should be back on my feet before long."

Before long. Ashley knew that was a doctor's euphemism for *I don't know how soon you can shake this.*

"How did things go?" Jill asked in her husky voice. "How's Davie?"

"The baby's fine," she answered, deciding to answer the easiest question first. "There's a young woman here who's great with the baby. Lily's her name. She'll be a great help to you."

"Are the people nice?" Jill asked anxiously.

"They seem anxious to make your stay a pleasant one," Ashley hedged. "I'll fill you in later. Right now, I want you to quit worrying and take care of yourself."

As they talked, Ashley moved restlessly around the room, not realizing that she was actually pacing from nervousness. She wanted to pour out her uneasiness about the whole situation, but she knew Jill wouldn't listen. She never did. Her twin was always making fun of the lack of adventure in Ashley's life, and chiding her for being such a stick-in-the-mud.

"Are there any good-looking men around?" Jill asked after heartily blowing her nose.

"Well, I've met one that will probably meet with your approval."

"What does he look like?"

Ashley thought for a moment. "I guess you could say he's a Pierce Brosnan look-alike."

"Wow," Jill croaked. "Not bad. Not bad."

"Did you meet a Kyle Stone when you were here?" Ashley asked, knowing that sooner or later her sister would get him in her sights, and Lily's sudden fear to talk about the man still worried her.

"The name doesn't ring a bell, but there were lots of guys hanging around Hugo. He could have been one of them, but if he's half as gorgeous as you say, I would have remembered him. Did he say he's met me?"

"No, but—" Ashley hesitated.

"But what? I can't see any reason for him not to remember me," she said with her usual lack of modesty. "You'll have to fill me in so I'll know what's gone on between you two."

Ashley decided not to pursue the subject until she had more than Lily's gossip to pass along. When Jill asked about the two children and her nanny duties, Ashley did her best to reassure her. "I'll know more after tomorrow. Don't worry, Jill. Just rest and get well."

After they'd said goodbye, Ashley put the phone

back in her purse, and closed the draperies. Then she checked on the baby and tried to relax as she got ready for bed.

STANDING AT THE WINDOW of the guest house, Kyle could look across the garden to the back of the house. The windows of the nursery and the adjoining bedroom were clearly visible, and his small but powerful binoculars brought Ashley's pacing figure sharply into focus.

"Damn," he swore when he saw that she was talking into a cell phone. He had been counting on being privy to every contact Jill made by phone. Every telephone in the house was bugged, and all phone conversations were recorded by an elaborate electronic set-up that he had hidden in a locked closet of the guest house. He couldn't believe he'd overlooked the possibility that she would bring a cell phone.

As he watched her in deep conversation with someone, he was chagrined that she'd outwitted him the first night. Vandenburg didn't tolerate sloppy work, and not knowing who she was contacting was a loose end that Kyle couldn't afford to let get by him. He'd have to get rid of that cell phone and quick.

As he watched her walk over and close the bedroom curtains, he wondered how soon it would be before she realized that she had a view of the guest cottage from her windows. Nothing about the time he'd spent with Jill had gone smoothly, and the knowledge that she could watch his coming and going from the guest house was less than reassuring. She wasn't nearly as self-centered as he'd been told.

He'd seen a flash of her temper when he'd made the mistake of following her up the stairs. Her flashing eyes and crisp tone had coldly dismissed him as if he'd been about to overstep some unspoken bound. In truth, he'd been hoping that they might end the night on a warmer note if they said goodnight at her bedroom door. The right words and tender looks could work wonders when it came to a satisfactory lingering parting with a woman. Everything about Jill's sexy looks should have encouraged a flirtation, but he'd struck out all evening with her.

After the lights went off in her room, he turned away from the window. Throwing himself down on the couch, he picked up the phone and made a call that he would just as soon have passed up if there'd been a choice.

ASHLEY HAD three and a half hours sleep before Davie woke up for his night feeding. She couldn't believe how loud a baby's demanding cry could sound in the middle of the night. Ignoring the infant's summons even for a few dazed moments wasn't an option. Groaning, she threw back a light cover and padded barefoot in her short summer gown into the nursery.

She knew the routine from taking care of the baby at her sister's. Fortunately, her diaper-changing time was improving. Even Davie seemed to be more patient with her less-than-experienced handling and her attempts to coax a smile from him. Everything was going well until she opened the door of the small refrigerator to get a bottle. The light suddenly went out, and the humming sound of the fridge cut off.

Somehow it had probably become unplugged, she thought, but Davie wasn't patient about waiting to be fed, so she put off checking the cord, and gave her attention to heating his bottle and feeding him.

Davie was content after his bottle, but not sleepy. She rocked him for nearly a half-an-hour before he finally went back to sleep and she could put him back in the crib.

The refrigerator was still dark and quiet, and even though it was small, she discovered that it was too heavy to pull out from the wall to check the plug.

"Nuts," she muttered. If it hadn't been for the two remaining bottles of formula, she wouldn't have been concerned, but she couldn't leave them in a warming fridge until morning. When Davie woke up in another four hours, there wouldn't be time to make up more formula. She had no choice. The bottles had to be refrigerated.

She put on a robe and slippers, and her clumsy fingers betrayed a nervousness just thinking about finding her way through a strange house to the kitchen in the dead of night.

The sitting room at the head of the stairs was in complete darkness, and muted moonlight failed to dispel eerie shapes which had lost their identity in the darkness. She stiffened as if some unseen danger lurked in the shadowy darkness, and she found herself listening for some betraying sound that someone might be watching her. It was as if some inner warning was trying to alert her to an unseen danger. She took a deep breath and firmly dismissed the intuitive feeling as utter foolishness. Just nervousness, she thought.

Her slippers made whispering noises on the marble floor downstairs, and even her breathing seemed to echo in the hushed stillness of the huge house. When she reached the end of the hall blocked by a series of French doors that opened on a dimly lit terrace, she knew she'd gone too far or turned too soon. All the halls and doors looked alike in the dead of night.

She paused for a moment and looked out one of the French doors. A quickening wind was whipping tree branches with fanatical glee, and the shadow of writhing palm leaves coming through the glass doors created weird images on the hall floor. The huge house with its vaulted ceilings suddenly seemed to engulf her, and an undefined sense of panic sluiced through her even as she chided herself for over-reacting. Feeling small and vulnerable, she fought off a nervous tightening in her chest. She vowed that tomorrow she would make herself a map of the house so she wouldn't be wandering around blind when she wanted to find her way around.

She finally located the family dining room and crossed it to the door that Gerta had used when she served dinner. It opened into a compact butler's pantry. The light from the dining room helped Ashley find the wall switch in the darkened serving room.

Looking around, Ashley saw that work counters, numerous cabinets and buffets took up most of the floor space. She paused a moment to appreciate several sets of china visible in the glass-doored cupboards and resisted a nagging temptation to open a drawer to see what antique silver tableware might be stored there. One of her graduate studies had focused on identifying period glass, porcelain and silver. Never in her life had she expected actually to see any of them.

Sighing, she pushed open a swinging door into the darkened kitchen. Her breath was slammed back down her throat as the glare of a flashlight caught her full force in the face. Before she knew what was happening, a giant hand reached out and grabbed her arm, knocking the baby bottles from her grasp.

She screamed, twisted around, trying to get free. In the struggle she glimpsed an enormous man, darkly bewhiskered, with a pockmarked nose and hard black eyes that sank deep in his head. Terror gave her strength she never knew she had. With one foot she lashed out at him with a savage force. He momentarily weakened the grip on her arm. She broke free.

Where to run? She'd lost her bearings. Where was the pantry door? Suddenly the kitchen's bright overhead light came on as the ape-like man flipped the switch and threw down his flashlight.

Ashley froze in terror as she saw the knife in his hand. The shiny blade was curved like a scimitar that could open up a stomach with one swipe. Her cries caught in her throat, swamped by pure fear.

At that moment, Kyle stormed through a back door into the kitchen. "Hendrick! What the hell are you doing?"

The cook waved his knife and shouted, "Nobody sneaks around my kitchen. Nobody."

"Put that damn knife down, Hendrick!" Kyle ordered. "Jill is a guest in this house."

"A guest," the cook snarled. "A guest who's checking out the loot in the middle of the night."

"Don't be stupid, Hendrick."

"The surveillance alarm in the pantry went off. I saw her clear as anything checking out the china and looking around."

The men's voices vibrated loudly in Ashley's ears. She couldn't find her voice, and, as Kyle's arm went around her waist, she felt her knees threatening to give way.

"You're out of your blasted mind, Hendrick! I'm going to report this to Hugo," Kyle said in a threatening tone, silently cursing the bombastic cook for creating the crisis. Blast it all! Hugo had left orders that Jill Gordon was to be handled with kid gloves, and there would be hell to pay if she packed up and left after one night in the house. The way she was leaning against him, he knew that she was fighting to keep from fainting.

"Go on, tell the boss." Hendrick snarled. "We'll see who's stupid." His glare was fierce enough to send another wave of weakness through Ashley.

At that moment, the kitchen suddenly filled up with people. Mrs. Borsch hurried in wearing a flannel robe, her long braid hanging down her back. Her thin, scowling husband was right behind her, hitching a pair of trousers over an undershirt. Lily and Gerta followed in nightclothes, their eyes round with surprise.

"What in God's name is going on in here?" the housekeeper demanded as her fiery eyes swept from the cook to Kyle and Ashley.

"It's her!" Hendrick jabbed a large-knuckled finger in Ashley's direction. "She was in the pantry, ready to loot the place. I told Hugo we ought to be keeping some of that silver in the safe. Maybe he'll listen to me now. Lucky I had the surveillance alarm and camera turned on. I caught her before she could get away with anything."

Ashley couldn't believe what she was hearing. For a moment, the cook's words failed to have any meaning. Shaken by the terror of his physical threats, she fought off a sense of unreality, as if she were somehow caught in a diabolical nightmare that would fade if she could just wake up.

"You're jumping to conclusions, Hendrick," Kyle said firmly. "It's just a misunderstanding," he said as if it were impossible that Jill could be guilty of casing out the pantry on her first night in the house. She surely wasn't that stupid. In fact, he'd just begun to think she was a lot more intelligent than rumors had given her credit for.

As Hendrick continued his accusing tirade, Ashley's emotional fog began to dissipate, and as indignation surged through her, she found her voice. "It's not true! I came downstairs to the kitchen with those!'' She pointed to the baby bottles on the floor. ''I had to put them in the fridge.''

''You have one in the nursery,'' Mrs. Borsch said coldly, as if Ashley's excuse was much too lame for an intelligent person to accept.

''Something's the matter with it!'' Ashley took a deep breath to lower the level of her voice. ''It stopped working, and I didn't want the last two bottles of formula to spoil. I knew there wouldn't be time to make more before Davie's next feeding.''

While Ashley was talking, Lily picked up the bottles from the floor. ''Lucky they're plastic,'' she said, as if that were the most important consideration at the moment.

The cook gave an ugly snort. ''You probably unplugged it yourself, just to have a reason for snooping around.''

Ashley glared at the cook. ''Why don't you come up to the nursery and check the fridge for yourself?''

''That's enough,'' Kyle snapped, and there was a warning in his tone. ''Let it go, Hendrick.''

Mrs. Borsch nodded. ''We can talk about this tomorrow. Joseph can check out the nursery refrigerator in the morning.''

Ashley couldn't tell whether her tone held a promise or a warning. Kyle turned to Ashley who had moved away from him as her anger at the cook had flared.

''Come on,'' he said. ''I'll see you upstairs.'' He nodded toward a door at one end of the kitchen. ''We can take the servants' back stairway. I'm sorry I didn't point it out to you earlier. You could have taken the stairs directly down to the kitchen.''

The way he said it made Ashley wonder if he really believed her story. Even though he had defended her, she had felt as if his protest of her innocence were somehow rehearsed. She suddenly felt uneasy with him and as he opened the door to a dimly lit staircase disappearing into a cavern of darkness above, a quiver of apprehension slithered up her back.

''I can find my way,'' she said quickly. ''No need to trouble yourself.''

''No trouble,'' Kyle assured her. Hell, she'd already played havoc with him trying to get some sleep. Restless and wandering around his small cottage, he had seen the lights in her bedroom and the nursery go on, and had decided she was feeding the baby. However, when the lights stayed on he started to get curious. Something was not right, and he'd learned from past experience that ignoring the unusual could be deadly.

He was on the stone walk leading from the guest cottage to the house when he'd heard her scream. Now she looked shaken and he could feel the trembling in her arm.

''It's all right,'' he assured her. ''There are lights all the way, but the stairs are narrow and you'll have to watch your step.''

Ashley started climbing upward in the narrow passage, taking the steps too fast because of her nervousness. In her haste, she misjudged the width of a step and stumbled.

His arms instantly went around her. "Steady does it."

"I'm fine," she said stiffly, trying to draw away from him. She wondered if he thought she'd engineered some kind of ploy to get in his arms. He must know that she was already indebted to him. Never in her life had she been more thankful than that moment when he'd stormed into the kitchen and stood between her and the manic cook.

"I'm really sorry," he said softly as they started upward again. This time he stayed on the same step with her, and kept a guiding hand on her arm as they moved upward together.

"You warned me about going in the kitchen when I wanted to express my appreciation to the cook. It's not your fault." She was angry with herself for getting into this situation. "I just didn't think."

As she trembled, his hand moved from her arm to around her waist. Through the clinging cloth of her short wrap-around robe and gown, Kyle could feel the ripple of her soft warm body as she moved beside him.

"I know Hendrick scared the heck out of you, and I'll have a talk with him. There was no cause for his stupidity. You'd think he owned the place the way he's suspicious of everyone. Nothing like this will happen again, I promise you."

"You can bet on that," she said firmly. If she were going to be here for much longer, there would be some battle lines drawn. Already she was wishing that she'd told Hendrick exactly what she thought of him and his guard-dog tactics.

"I have the feeling that you'll not back down from Hendrick, or anyone else," Kyle said.

Ashley detected an edge of surprise in his tone that bordered on reluctant admiration. She was totally aware of his embrace and the brush of his hard thighs against hers in the close quarters. Could he hear the pounding of her heart? she wondered, trying to ignore the effect his nearness was having on her. *I'm just vulnerable right now,* she told herself, and for a moment allowed herself to lean into his protective strength.

"It's just a little farther," he assured her, keeping his arm around her waist. "I didn't realize you might be afraid of dark places."

She started to assure him that it wasn't the dark, narrow staircase that had sent her emotions reeling, but thought better of it. Let him think what he would.

When they reached the top of the stairs, he opened a door to the second-floor hall. "This is it. We're at the opposite end of the hall from your rooms."

When they reached the sitting room at the top of the main staircase, she said, "Thank you. I know my way from here."

Kyle smiled at her prim dismissal. No doubt about it, she'd been shaken by what had happened in the kitchen, and he admired the way she had pulled herself together. For a few brief moments on the staircase, he had felt a struggle going on within her, but in the end she'd shown her inner strength and pulled herself together. In the stairwell, he'd found himself drawn to much more than her courage. Her nearness had teased him with inviting femininity. He had wanted to pull her close and let his lips trail along her sweet neck as she leaned back against him. For a tempting instant, he had almost let his hands slip from her waist down to the rounded smoothness of her hips and thighs. Even now he fought the rising heat of desire as he watched her walk quickly down the hall away from him.

Don't be a fool, he told himself. There was no quicker way to put a noose around his own neck than to have romantic feelings for Jill Gordon.

Chapter Five

Ashley awoke with a groan when Davie announced to the world it was time for a dry diaper and a bottle. Sleep had evaded her until almost dawn. The adrenaline that had poured through her body lingered, keeping her muscles tense and her nerves taut as piano wires. Her thoughts kept forming and changing like a kaleidoscope as she tossed this way and another in the bed. It seemed that she had just slipped away into sleep when the baby's demanding cries awakened her.

As she lifted her head from the pillow, she'd never felt so completely drained, physically and emotionally. How was she going to cope? The challenges facing her on this first day with the children were of nightmare proportions. She had always prided herself on painstaking lesson plans and hours of careful preparation before any teaching assignment. Even though Pamela and Benny were just children, keeping them interested in learning was probably a bigger challenge than with her college students. She hadn't even looked at their schoolbooks to familiarize herself with their level of instruction.

"All I have to do is mark time," Ashley told herself. Her sister was the one who would be taking over the job in a few days. No use setting up any elaborate lesson plans that Jill would ignore. She went into the nursery and cooed at Davie as she lifted him from his crib. He was bright-eyed and happy for a brief moment as she cuddled him in her arms, but as soon as she laid him down on the changing table, he waved his arms and kicked impatiently as if he were bicycling.

"All right, all right," she laughed at his babyish antics. "I get the message."

Then her eyes fell on the silent refrigerator, and the ordeal of going back down to the kitchen to get a bottle swept over her. She was blaming herself for not making arrangements for Lily to bring a bottle when there was a light knock on the nursery door.

Ashley's heart leapt with hope. "Come in." Like an angel of mercy, the smiling, redheaded Lily came in with a breakfast tray. Ashley wanted to hug and kiss her, but settled for a prayerful, "Thank you, Lily."

As the young maid's clear brown eyes passed over Ashley's tousled hair and worried expression, she said, "I was thinking you might want a bite in your room this morning. The kids are already at breakfast and I brought a warm bottle for Davie. Would you like for me to feed him while you have some toast, fruit and coffee? I wasn't quite sure what else you might be wanting.'' She eyed Ashley's trim figure. ''I was thinking you probably didn't eat all that much any time, but I can fill a plate from the breakfast buffet if you'd like.''

''No, thank you. This will be fine,'' Ashley assured her.

''Good. I'll just set the tray down on your bedside table.'' She whisked into the bedroom and back. ''Now let me have that little one. I told Benny and Pamela to wait for you in the library when they finished breakfast. Mrs. Borsch was on the warpath this morning.'' She glanced at Ashley and swallowed back whatever she was about to say.

No doubt, the fiasco last night had put the housekeeper in a bad mood, thought Ashley. She'd already warned her that she didn't like her sleep interrupted. ''I'm sorry about last night,'' Ashley said wearily.

Lily shrugged. ''Not your fault. Besides that isn't what set her off. I heard Mr. Stone having words with Mrs. Borsch, something about making up one of the guest rooms. I guess Mr. Vandenburg sent word that there's going to be another visitor arriving in a couple of days.'' Lily sighed. ''That'll mean more work for all of us.''

''Who is it? Do you know?'' Ashley's chest suddenly tightened. What if it was someone who knew Jill? Would her twin be well enough to make the switch before the visitor got here? ''A couple of days?'' Ashley prodded.

She nodded. ''Mr. Stone didn't seem too happy about it.''

"I wonder why," Ashley said, thinking aloud.

Lily shrugged. "Beats me."

Ashley didn't have time to think any more about this new complication. She was already engulfed in the constantly mounting challenge of being someone she wasn't.

Hurrying through breakfast, she showered and dressed in a white blouse and flamboyant floral skirt. Grabbing up the children's schoolbooks and putting a few things in a white pouch purse, she hurried downstairs, relieved to find the library doors open, so she didn't have to hunt and peek to find the right room.

"Good morning," she said as she crossed the room to the leather couch. Benny was slouching at one end and Pamela was sitting primly at the other. Both children looked up at her with trapped expressions as she sat down in a chair opposite them. "I'm sorry I'm late."

Benny groaned when he saw the schoolbooks in her hands. "Jeez," he muttered. "What a bummer."

"He hates books," Pamela said, scowling at her brother. "The only thing he likes is airplanes, airplanes, airplanes."

"Have you read any exciting books about airplanes, Benny?"

"Naw. I can't find any good ones for kids."

"Well, why don't you write one?"

"Me? You're out of your gourd."

"Maybe not," Ashley smiled as Pamela looked at her brother in total disgust, obviously sure that Benny was in trouble with the new nanny already. "You could tell about your airplanes and even draw some pictures to illustrate it."

"I hate writing, all that spelling and punctuation stuff," he scoffed. "Pammy's the one who writes stories." He slouched down farther on the couch.

"I tell you what, Benny. I'll be your secretary. How would that be? You can tell me about your planes, and I'll type what you say on the computer for you. That way you'll have your own book that you can read to your mother and father." She smiled at Pamela. "And I bet you could write an exciting story about a girl like yourself. Maybe someone who wins all kinds of medals for swimming. Do you want to try? When you're finished I could type yours, too."

A shiny glint in Pamela's eyes told Ashley that she'd hit pay dirt. "I'm good at writing stories."

"Terrific," Ashley said as she rose to her feet and started toward the computer desk. "I'll type Benny's story while you write yours, Pamela. And then while he's drawing his airplanes, we can decide what kinds of pictures would go best with yours. Okay, let's get to work."

WHEN KYLE peeked in the library door later in the morning, he was astonished to see the two children huddled around their new nanny and the computer. Their rapt attention was a total surprise. He didn't know what they were up to, but he was relieved that Jill seemed to have the situation under control. When she hadn't shown up for breakfast, he'd feared that last night's debacle might have sent her packing, but things were looking up. She must really need this job as badly as Hugo had surmised.

Was she desperate for money? Kyle didn't want to think that she had been casing the house last night for valuables that might be turned into cash, but the possibility lingered. Budge had proven to be a clever thief, and maybe his wife was cut from the same cloth. Kyle knew better than to be blinded by her charms. The first thing he needed to do was to find her damn cell phone and fix it so she'd have to make calls on the house phones.

While she was busy with the kids in the library it was a good time. He hurried upstairs to the nursery and greeted Lily with a warm, "How are things going, pretty lady?"

Color rose in Lily's cheeks as Kyle smiled at her. Davie was in a playpen, staring up at a musical mobile and waving his arms as if wanting more than anything to reach up and grab the hanging trinkets.

"Everything's fine," she assured him. "The refrigerator had a frayed cord that must have shorted out. Joseph replaced it, and I made up some fresh bottles."

So she was telling the truth—or else she'd damaged the cord herself.

"Why don't you take the fellow for a little fresh air in the stroller?" Kyle casually suggested to Lily. "I bet you wouldn't mind getting out of the house for a bit yourself."

Her brown eyes brightened. "Do you think that would be all right, taking the baby out like that?"

"Of course."

In just a few minutes Lily had left the house with the baby, and he was free to search for the cell phone. Putting it out of order would be no trick at all. He only needed a few seconds to drop some liquid glue under the number keys so they wouldn't function.

The bedroom was a lot neater than he would have expected. She had already made her bed, hung up all her clothes, including the red dress and her nightwear from last night, and her cosmetics were laid out neatly on a mirrored dressing table. The lingering scent of her perfume triggered a sexual attraction that he'd been trying to deny ever since their physical closeness in the stairwell, and he jerked his mind back to the task at hand. He knew better than to let any stupid fantasies interfere with his job. Sure, she was temptation enough for any red-blooded man, but if he didn't find the phone there'd be hell to pay when Hugo found out she'd made contact with someone her first night in the house.

When he couldn't find the phone lying out in the open, he started looking through all the drawers, careful not to disturb the order of the contents. The sensual fragrance of her lingerie challenged his determination to stay immune from her feminine appeal. After moving from the dressing table to the five-drawer bureau and not finding anything, he opened a sliding door to the closet, and saw two suitcases on a shelf. He hurriedly checked them. Nothing.

His eyes swept the room, and he saw a small cosmetic case sitting on the shelf of a stand. When he opened it, he knew that he had hit pay dirt—a cell phone.

He worked quickly, putting glue under the dial numbers to make it inoperable. Then he placed the phone back in the small case and returned it to the nightstand's shelf. Satisfied that she wouldn't be able to use the cell again, he quickly left the bedroom and made his way back downstairs.

When he entered the library, both Pamela and Benny rushed toward him and started talking at once.

''We're making our own books.''

''See! It's got pictures.''

''We're going to put fancy covers on them, aren't we, Jill?''

Kyle laughed and gave Benny's head a Dutch rub and Pamela's shoulder an affectionate pat. ''Whoa! What do we have here? A couple of budding authors?''

''You can read them when we're finished,'' Pamela promised.

Kyle smiled at Ashley. ''Sounds as if you've got a handle on these kids already.'' He hoped his words didn't hint at his surprise. Their enthusiasm was completely unexpected.

''They've worked so hard I think we'll quit for the morning,'' Ashley said, signing off on the computer.

''Great idea.'' Kyle agreed, glancing at his watch. ''How about an hour's swim, kids, before lunch?'' As they heralded their approval, he turned to Ashley. ''You'll enjoy the indoor Olympic-size pool.''

"Oh, I think I'd better relieve Lily with the baby—" she started to protest.

"Lily decided to take Davie out for a little fresh air in his stroller. This is a great time for you to work up an appetite for lunch and relax a little bit."

He had one more thing on his agenda. Her white purse was lying on top of the schoolbooks, and he guessed that she would take it with her to the pool, since most women never went anywhere without their pocketbooks. He knew his best chance for getting his hand on it would be while she was in the pool. He needed to search her purse for any clues that might indicate that she'd been in contact with her husband.

"Come on, Jilly," Benny coaxed.

Jilly? For a moment, the nickname shocked Ashley. Then she laughed, realizing that she must have passed some test with the little boy if he'd given her a pet name.

"Will you time my laps?" Pamela asked her. "I'm getting faster all the time."

"Well, what do you say, Jilly?" Kyle gave her a conspirator's wink as he used the nickname. "How about I meet you guys at the pool in ten minutes?"

"All right," she agreed. Exercise would ease some of the tension she'd been under during the teaching session, and also the leftover anxiety from last night. She still couldn't believe how well the morning had gone. Thank goodness she'd remembered a teacher friend of hers who taught at the elementary level telling her about the success her class had had making their own books. The memory of that conversation had surfaced just in time. This was a project that Jill could manage. And what was more important, she'd have something to show Mr. Vandenburg when he checked up on her.

She felt Kyle's eyes following her down the hall as she and the children went upstairs to get their bathing suits. Maybe this wasn't such a good idea, after all, she worried, having second thoughts. Parading around in Jill's skimpy bikini bathing suit might invite the kind of intimacy that she was trying to avoid. One thing was sure, she'd have to stay away from him in the pool. The memory of his nearness on the stairs was enough to warn her about any further physical contact, and seeing the drop-dead handsome Mr. Stone in bathing trunks promised to be enough of a challenge in itself.

As quickly as she could, she slipped into Jill's hot pink bikini, grateful for a matching floral sarong. She grabbed a towel and rubber thongs from the bathroom, and hurried down the hall to the sitting room where the children were waiting impatiently.

"Benny wanted to go on ahead but I told him you probably didn't know the way," Pamela said in her big-sister tone.

"Thank you, Pammy," Ashley said using the little girl's nickname deliberately. There was a lonely wistfulness about her that had already touched Ashley's heart.

"You don't take towels," Benny told Ashley in a tone that said she'd better depend upon him and not his big sister to set her straight about things.

"Oh, really. Well, I guess I'll have an extra one then," Ashley said, smiling. "I'm glad I have you two to show me where to go and what to do."

Benny stuck out his little chest. "Just follow me, Jilly." With that he bounded down the stairs like a young mountain goat and waited impatiently at the bottom for Ashley and his sister to follow.

Neither of the children seemed aware of Mrs. Borsch's cold stare when they met the housekeeper in the hall, but Ashley felt a censoring glare as well as a scowl of new displeasure.

"Have you misplaced the daily schedule, Mrs. Gordon?" she asked with the crispness of an ice cutter. "I believe swimming is an activity for the afternoon, and the children are supposed to have studies in the library until lunch."

"We finished up early today," Ashley said, automatically falling back on the demeanor of a college professor. She was accustomed to making decisions about the length of her lectures and class periods. "I decided that a swim before lunch would be a reward for the hard work they did this morning."

Mrs. Borsch's bony cheeks flushed. "You were hired to carry out Mr. Vandenburg's wishes, and he has laid out a daily schedule which you are expected to follow."

"You're not our boss!" Benny lashed out with a pugnacious set of his chin. "Kyle said we could go swimming, so there!"

The housekeeper looked as if she wanted to reach out and cuff him for such impertinence, but her clenched hands stayed at her side. "Then I'll be speaking to Mr. Stone," she said, and with one last withering glare at Ashley walked stiffly away.

A spacious glassed-in swimming pool was at the end of a narrow hall just beyond the solarium. Ashley noted that there were several dressing rooms at one end of the lounging area, and when Kyle emerged from one, she wished she'd waited to put on her bathing suit. She was self-conscious parading back and forth through the house in Jill's bathing suit and draped sarong.

Kyle picked up a beach towel from a pile on a counter, and tossed it on a nearby lounge chair. As he moved toward her with a masculine grace that rippled muscles in his lightly tanned body, Ashley knew her suspicion about the way he looked in bathing trunks was correct. Knock-down gorgeous. Never in her life had she felt so vulnerable to the seductive magnetism of a masculine physique.

"Ready for a swim?" he asked, as his gaze traveled over her bare shoulders and the soft floral material hugging her nearly naked body.

As his eyes undressed her, she wanted to turn and run. She'd been a fool to get herself into a situation like this. Outgoing, spontaneous friendliness came easily to Jill, but not to Ashley, and now she was faced with acting the way her twin would if she were going swimming with Kyle Stone.

"Last one in is a turkey!" Benny sang out as he dove into the pool, and began to dog paddle with boyish glee.

"Don't pay any attention to him," Pamela scoffed.

Ashley and Kyle watched as she made her way to the diving board at the deep end. Very precisely, the young girl stepped to the end, put her arms in position over her head, and with a practiced ease made a beautiful swan dive into the water.

"She's very good," smiled Ashley.

Kyle nodded. "Shall we join them?"

Careful, now, Ashley told herself. Even though her sister was a good swimmer, Jill scarcely got her suit wet at beach parties. She preferred to lounge around the pool, or sit on the edge, dangling her feet. In contrast, Ashley had spent as much time in the college pool as she could. She would have loved to join Pamela on the diving board and swim laps with her, but she knew better. "It's a beautiful pool," Ashley said honestly, appreciating the beautiful aquamarine tile that lined the pool and matched the mosaic design on the walls.

Putting her purse and towel on a chair, she quickly untied the wrap-around, walked over to steps leading down into the pool and lowered herself into the water.

Kyle watched her, and the view of her supple body in the vivid pink bikini was tantalizing enough to raise any man's testosterone level. In spite of himself, he mentally cupped the rounded firmness of her fanny with his hands, and caressed full breasts tugging at the narrow string around her neck. Fantasizing about what it would be like to have the length of that luscious body pressed against his sent a sudden warmth sluicing through him. He struggled to control his wayward thoughts before the tight fit of his swimming trunks betrayed his imagination.

As she sliced through the water with natural grace, Kyle jumped off the side of the pool near where Benny was splashing around in the water. All the time he was horsing around with the boy, he kept his eye on Jill and Pamela who were swimming in the deep end.

"I forgot my fins," Benny said, and started dog-paddling toward the edge of the pool.

"I'll get them for you," Kyle said quickly, moving quickly past him with a strong breast stroke, and then easily lifting himself up onto the side of the pool.

"I left them in the shower room the last time," Benny called. "And get the beach ball, too."

Kyle made an okay sign with his hand. Getting to his feet, he picked up his towel where he had dropped it, and then he sat down on a lounge chair next to the one where Ashley had set her white purse. Very deliberately, he dried himself off, and then as he bent over to slip into his thongs, he tossed his towel on the next chair, covering the white purse. When he got up, he picked up his towel with the purse underneath and headed into the dressing room and showers. Quickly closing the door he congratulated himself on a job well done.

As he went through the bag, he found everything that a woman might carry around, including a red leather wallet and key case. His dexterous fingers flipped through the wallet, checking the driver's license, photos of the baby and a handsome one of

Budge in his basketball uniform. Interesting, thought Kyle. Despite her husband's desertion and criminal activities, Jill had kept his picture in her wallet.

His hopes of finding any letters, notes or correspondence were not realized. Two one-hundred-dollar bills were tucked under one of the photo pockets, and about fifty dollars in smaller bills in the money compartment. What was puzzling to him was that there were neither credit cards nor checkbooks.

He could hear the kids squealing and splashing, and knew he had to get back to the pool before one of them came looking for him. The search had been disappointing. He wasn't sure what he had hoped to find, but he would have thought that someone like Jill would have collected a bunch of purse litter that might have told him something.

Concealing the purse in his towel again, he hurried into the shower room, picked up Benny's fins and the beach ball. Trying to hold everything and keep the purse covered wasn't an easy task, but he managed.

He threw the beach ball out at the three bobbing heads, and as they raced for it, he quickly set the purse on the towel that Jill had brought with her. He'd never been a good loser, and he couldn't get rid of an intuitive feeling that somehow a blue-eyed temptress had made a fool out of him.

"Keep Away! Boys against girls," Pamela announced with a confident smile at Ashley as Kyle jumped back in the pool.

"Come on, Kyle, we'll show 'em," Benny bragged as he grabbed the ball. Pamela made a grab for the ball, but it was already in the air. Kyle easily caught it over Ashley's head and sent it back.

Amid splashing and kicking, the ball lobbed back and forth, sometimes between the fellows and sometimes between Pamela and Ashley. They were playing in the middle of the pool until Benny gave the ball a wild toss that carried it into deep water. Both Kyle and Ashley went for it as the kids screamed for their partner to get there first.

With kicking feet and outstretched hands Ashley and Kyle fought for the ball. There was no way to avoid body contact as they splashed about in the water. As the slippery ball kept moving away from them, they found themselves entangled in each other's arms and legs. Kyle captured her in his firm arms and laughingly held her back from the ball.

Stubbornly, she tried to take it from him, and as he felt the softness of her nearly naked, utterly feminine body entwined with his, the challenge of the game was lost. Crystal droplets of water sparkled on her crescent eyelashes and the lovely curves of her lips. A demanding desire surged through him.

She stared at him with rounded eyes before he loosened his grip and let her slip away.

"That's enough," she said and threw the ball out of the pool. Then she quickly climbed up the side ladder. "Come on, kids, it's almost lunchtime."

Ashley urged Pamela and Benny out of the pool, completely ignoring Kyle. She grabbed her towel, gave her body a quick once-over and then wrapped the sarong around her. She knew she was running away. What had nearly happened in the pool was nothing short of disaster.

As his possessive touch had slipped over her nearly naked body, she'd seen the desire in his eyes. It appalled her that she had responded to it. For one insane moment she'd forgotten herself and had wanted him to kiss her. Only an unbidden protective urge deep within rescued her as she raised her legs and pushed him away.

"Hurry," she urged Pamela and Benny. "Mrs. Borsch will be upset if we're late for lunch." As quickly as she could, she helped them dry off and slip into their long T-shirts and thongs. "We can shower and change upstairs."

"Aren't you coming, Kyle?" Benny called to him.

"I think I'll do some laps first." *And then take a nice cold shower,* he added silently.

Ashley still felt heat rising in her as she glanced back at him in the water, shocks of raven hair drifting down on his forehead as he watched her.

Chapter Six

Ashley herded the children ahead of her down the hall, past the solarium. When she saw Joseph and Hendrick staring at her through the windows, she knew that she'd made a mistake by not using the dressing rooms instead of parading around in a damp sarong.

Both men deliberately gave her the once-over and then Joseph said something that brought a smirk to both their faces. She was both angry and embarrassed as she gave a lift to her head and tried to ignore a defenseless vulnerability rising within her. She felt as if she were making a mess that her sister was going to have to clean up.

"Fifteen minutes and we have to be downstairs," Ashley warned as the children bounded toward their rooms. She knew that Lily was scheduled to stay with the baby until after lunch. Then Ashley would have Davie until three o'clock when physical activities were scheduled. She knew that she'd fouled up the first day by agreeing to Kyle's suggestion of a swim before lunch. From now on, she'd make sure that he didn't take charge of her or the children.

In the nursery, Lily asked her how things had gone with the children that morning. Ashley just said, "Fine. How did you and Davie get along?"

"He's a real joy, he is. You're a lucky mother," she said with an edge of envy.

Ashley bent over the sleeping baby and was filled with emotion. No matter what kind of a mess Jill had made marrying Budge, this beautiful little boy made it all worthwhile. Ashley felt a rare rush of envy, and for the first time was grateful that she was having a part in their lives. This was going to be a good place for Davie to spend the first few months of his life— *if I don't ruin it for him.* Guilty thoughts about her behavior in the pool made her voice brusque as she turned away from the crib.

"I've got to change for lunch. I'll be back up as soon as I can," she promised Lily.

"Don't be hurrying. Mrs. Borsch will just be finding me a hundred things to do when I go downstairs."

Ashley went into her bathroom, showered and then looked in the closet for something to put on. She took a green silk pantsuit off a hanger and slipped into it. As she sat on the bed putting on some matching sandals, her gaze fell on a piece of paper on the floor.

She bent over and picked it up. After a quick glance, she realized it was a receipt from the hairdresser who had styled her hair like Jill's. Ashley remembered shoving it into her cosmetic bag when she'd been packing. How did it get on the floor? It hadn't been there when she'd dressed earlier in the day or she would have noticed it.

Puzzled, she looked inside the cosmetic case. There wasn't much in it because she'd put all of Jill's cosmetics on the dresser. The only thing stored in the case was her Colorado cell phone. Since she was using Jill's phone, she'd decided to leave hers there, and last night, after talking to her twin, she'd put Jill's phone under her pillow instead of returning it to the cosmetic case.

Ashley's hands tightened on the green sandal and suddenly her mouth was parched. There was only one way the receipt could have gotten on the floor from her cosmetic bag.

Someone had been going through her things.

Lily was the one who had the most opportunity to go through her belongings, reasoned Ashley, but as far as she could tell nothing was missing. The jewelry she'd brought was still in a dressing-table drawer, and Jill's supply of cosmetics was complete. Maybe the young maid was just nosey. That must be it. No harm done. Lily was the most pleasant of anyone in the house, and Ashley wasn't going to say anything to her. She was just young enough to give in to her curiosity and poke about to see what she could see.

A hesitant knock on her door told Ashley that the children were ready for lunch. As she gave one last glance in the mirror to check the tight, tapered lime-green slacks and matching midriff top, she had the weird sensation that Jill was frowning back at her, none too pleased with the mess she was making of things.

"I'm doing my best," Ashley said to her own reflection, and then quickly turned away before she could see the doubt in her shadowed blue eyes.

Kyle didn't show up for lunch, which was the first blessing of the day, decided Ashley. Maybe she was just too naive, but she wasn't ready to pretend that nothing out of the ordinary had passed between them.

Both Pamela and Benny were tired from their hour of swimming and didn't protest when Ashley told them to find something quiet to do in their rooms until three o'clock.

She settled on map-making for the afternoon's activity. Carrying paper and drawing pens, they made their way down to the beach.

"This is dumb," Benny grumbled. "How can we make a map of this place?"

Ashley directed their attention to the irregular coastline and let them climb up on a mound of rocks so they could see the way reefs formed a natural cove. "If you were a pirate captain bringing your ship into shore, Benny, you'd need to know where the reefs are and the best place to berth your ship. Why don't you draw a map that shows you all of that?"

His scowl turned into a grin. Without any further protest, he drew a skull and crossbones at the top of his paper.

Pamela chewed on her pencil for a moment. "Can I make a map to show the shape of the whole island? Did you know Roble Island is shaped like a chili pepper?"

"No, I didn't know that. Great idea." Ashley

agreed. "You can even mark where your grandfather's house is."

Pamela nodded and went happily to work.

Ashley was pleased that the drawing lesson was going well. She'd found a book in the library about the early settlers of the island and decided that map drawing might make tomorrow's history lesson a little more relevant.

As the children drew, she let her gaze follow the white sandy beach in both directions. Some distance away, a small boathouse and dock were the only structures on the Vandenburg private beach, but no boats were visible and there was a deserted look about the whole scene.

KYLE COULDN'T figure out what the kids were drawing. As far as he could tell, there was nothing to be seen but rolling surf. He had kept his distance when they left the house, not wanting to alert Jill that she was being watched. If she knew that she was on a tight leash, she might try to cover her movements.

He stayed out of sight in a thick drift of palmetto trees above the rocks where they were sitting. Her laughter and the childish chatter of the children drifted up to him, and he had an absurd desire to join them. How would she react? The biting memory of the way she'd fled from him at the pool kept him sitting where he was.

When they left the beach and made their way back to the house, he decided that the outing hadn't had any hidden design. Undoubtedly she'd tell him at dinner what the project had been about.

Only she didn't come down to dinner. Lily took a dinner tray up to her, and he had to be content with watching her from his cottage.

The next morning, she had breakfast with the children and disappeared into the library. When Kyle heard from Lily what was in the works for the afternoon's activity, an alarm went off.

"She's taking the children for a drive around the island," Lily told him. "Got maps and some stuff from the library about the history of the place." She chuckled. "Sounds like she wants to know as much about Roble Island as somebody writing a book about the place."

Kyle managed to keep a smile on his face while his thoughts raced. What in the hell was she up to? One thing was sure, he'd bet his bottom dollar that Jill Gordon wasn't getting the lay of Roble Island in order to write any book. "How long ago did they leave?"

"About a half hour."

It took Kyle about an hour to locate the white Mercedes parked in the museum lot. For some reason, he had expected her to take Beachview Drive, edging the Atlantic side of Roble Island.

He was almost positive that the outing was just a ruse. He trusted Jill Gordon about as much as he did her fugitive husband. She was a smart one. Under the guise of teaching the children about the island, she had a free rein to go anywhere she wanted. It was a double game they were playing, and Kyle sure as hell didn't intend to lose.

He went inside the museum to take a quick look to see if they were really there. When they were nowhere in sight, he was sure she'd conned him. As casually as he could he approached the teenage girl at the ticket desk.

"I guess I missed my party." He smiled at her. "Maybe you can help me? A pretty honey-blond lady with two children, a boy and girl?"

She returned his smile, and smoothed a dangling strand of hair as if she wanted to appear her best. "Oh, yes, I think they left a few minutes ago."

He frowned. "I was supposed to meet them at the car, and it's still in the parking lot."

"Oh, I heard them talking about walking down to the harbor," she told him, eager to be of help. "It's just a short way to the wharf and shops."

As if he didn't know the island like the back of his hand, he said, "Thank you very much."

ASHLEY AND THE CHILDREN finished their sugary treat and continued to sit on the park bench watching the panorama of people, boats and diving seagulls. They had about ten minutes to wait for the excursion boat, and the children were tossing some crumbs to some scavenger seagulls a short distance away when Ashley suddenly felt a sense of uneasiness.

For a moment, what was causing the psychic reaction didn't register, until she realized that a tall, swarthy-faced man, darkly dressed, was standing on the sidewalk a few feet away, looking at her.

Her chest tightened. Something about the intensity of his stare sent a warning through her. Even though she'd never had the experience of being stalked, a sensation of being the focus of a crazed mind surged through her. A knowing glint in the man's ferret eyes and the half-smile on his thick lips sent a bone-deep shiver through her.

He came toward her, and as he stopped directly in front of her, she instinctively pressed back against the hardness of the bench to put as much distance between them as she could.

"Jill...Jill Gordon, isn't it?"

Her first reaction was to emphatically deny it. Her frozen expression must have betrayed her inner confusion. How could she pretend to know this man when just looking at him made her skin crawl? She couldn't find her voice to say anything.

"I guess you don't remember me?" The lines in his ugly, bony face deepened and his intense small eyes narrowed.

"No, I'm afraid I don't," she answered with great effort, wondering what on earth her sister had to do with a sleazy-looking character like this man.

"Rudy Dietz."

He held out a hand, which she ignored. Just looking at his hairy hand and blackened fingernails made her skin crawl. There was no way she was going to let him touch her.

He dropped his arm, shrugged as his mouth spread

in a mocking grin that showed large, uneven teeth. "So that's how it is. Well, then, until we meet again. Maybe your memory will improve with time. Good day, Mrs. Gordon." He gave her a mock bow, turned and walked away.

Ashley sat stunned. She couldn't believe the man's approach had been a casual one. Something about his predatory manner reeked of cold, deliberate purpose.

Glancing at her watch, she took a deep breath, rose to her feet and motioned for the children who had been too busy chasing birds to notice the unpleasant stranger. "It's time to catch the boat."

As Benny and Pamela bounced ahead of her down the waterfront sidewalk, she regretted the promised boat ride. The afternoon's outing had been spoiled. At the moment, she would have preferred to return to the house. Tense, worried and jittery, she couldn't get rid of the feeling that she was being watched and followed. *Please don't let that man get on the boat with us,* she prayed.

They had almost reached the correct dock when she realized someone was coming up behind her, and before she could turn around, a hand touched her shoulder. A scream caught in her throat as she spun around.

"Oh, it's you," she choked when she saw Kyle, feeling relieved and angry at the same time.

"Hey, I'm sorry if I startled you," he apologized quickly, seeing her expression of total fright.

"It's...it's all right." She quickly composed herself.

He wanted to ask her why she was so uptight, but

from the firm lift of her head, he knew that the moment had already passed when she might tell him why she was tense and defensive.

Who did she think he was?

Someone she was expecting?

Now that her initial scare was over, she seemed relieved to see him.

"We're going down the island on a boat," Pamela said, her eyes flashing with excitement.

"Want to come with us, Kyle?" Benny invited. "It'll be a blast."

"Sure, why not?" he readily agreed. "I just finished doing a little shopping for Hendrick." He smiled at Ashley. "You don't mind if I crash the party, do you?"

Her eyes quickly searched the dock area, and came back to him with a feeling of relief. The ugly man was nowhere in sight. "Not at all."

"Good. I'll get the tickets." He knew it wasn't his company that made her readily agree to his joining them. Jill Gordon was anxious to avoid someone.

Once aboard, they took outside seats at the back of the excursion boat. The children chatted and pointed at passing docks and marinas along the shoreline. A clean, brisk wind touched their faces and ruffled their hair as ribbons of white wake spread out behind them.

Kyle glanced over the heads of the two children sitting between them and saw that a faint smile had replaced the tense lines of Jill's lovely mouth.

Good, he thought. She'd accepted his presence without suspicion. Now all he had to do was keep his eyes open and figure out why it might be important for her to know the beaches and coves of the island. He was sure she had arranged this boat excursion down to the tip of the island to scout out a meeting place with Budge.

As the boat chugged southward, Ashley found the passing shoreline a fascinating mixture of beaches, marshlands and forests. And, as they rounded the southern tip of the island, her interest was caught by an old abandoned lighthouse standing in dense undergrowth like a proud sentinel of the past.

Like so many other historians, she was fascinated by lighthouses because most of them had myriad romantic tales woven into their pasts. She wondered if there might be a book in the library about this one. It didn't look as if it had become an historical site like some that had been preserved. It looked abandoned.

She asked Kyle if the lighthouse was open to the public.

"No, I don't think so."

"Too bad," she said. "I would love to see it up close."

He almost said, Who's kidding who? Did she really expect him to believe her interest in an old lighthouse was for real?

Benny pointed excitedly. "Is that Grandfather's house?"

Kyle nodded as a glimpse of the white mansion was seen through a forest of trees edging down to the water. "Sure is. He owns all of the beach from here to the yacht club."

"Wow," Benny breathed.

"Your grandfather is a very rich man."

"I know," sighed Pamela. "I just wish I liked him better."

He's a hard man to like, Kyle said to himself. Hugo Vandenburg never did anything without an ulterior motive, and Jill Gordon was fooling herself if she thought she was living here out of the goodness of his heart. *She'll learn to dance to his tune like the rest of us,* he thought, and entertained a moment of regret before he shoved the thought away. There was more at stake here than worrying about Jill Gordon's feelings.

The boat turned around and headed back up the coast to the harbor, and Ashley felt her chest tighten again. What if the horrid man was still hanging around?

She glanced at Kyle, wondering if she should say something to him? No, she couldn't. He might start asking her questions about Jill's friends and acquaintances.

"What is it?" Kyle asked as he caught her questioning eyes upon him.

"Do you live on Roble Island all year round?"

His guard went up. He didn't know where the question came from, but what he did with his time wasn't open to casual chitchat. "Oh, I come and go as Mr. Vandenburg needs me," he said with a dismissing wave of his hand. "The boss thought I might help you and the children settle in."

"We like Jilly," Benny broke in as if his opinion counted for something. "Don't let Grandfather send her away."

"Not much chance of that." Kyle laughed to hide the truth in the assurance.

Ashley sensed that there was something more behind his casual remark. Was Jill right in thinking that Hugo was befriending her, or was there some less noble reason he had offered her the nanny job?

When the boat pulled into port, Ashley stayed at Kyle's side as they waited for their turn to exit. Her eyes searched the waiting crowd, but she didn't see the stranger who had taken her for her twin.

"Where are you parked?" Ashley asked, wishing she'd brought the car down to the wharf instead of leaving it at the museum.

"Behind the Beachfront Inn. How about you?" he asked with practiced innocence as if he didn't know.

"At the museum. Would you mind dropping us off there? It's getting late, and I should get the children back so they can have a little rest before dinner."

"Sure. Come on."

As Benny and Pamela dived ahead of them through the milling crowd, Kyle was surprised at how closely she kept at his side as they walked to his car. When he put a guiding hand on her arm, she didn't protest. In fact, she seemed grateful for it. What was going on? She'd let him know in more ways than one that she wanted him to keep his distance. This contradiction in her behavior puzzled him, and her request to drive them a few blocks to her car seemed contrived.

Was she frightened of something? Or someone?

As they headed down the narrow road toward the museum in his car, he asked smoothly, "Well, did you enjoy your first look at the island?"

She nodded, but he glimpsed a tightening in her cheeks that didn't go with her polite smile.

"I've always found museums to be rather boring," he said, trying to keep the conversation going. "Maybe I just didn't have the right company. If you and the kids go again, maybe I can tag along."

"I'm sorry I didn't invite you today," she said with a sincerity that surprised him. "I'm glad we ran into you."

"Me, too." He was sure that something had gone wrong with the day's plans, but what? Maybe something had happened at the museum that he needed to know about. Had she met someone? Or received a message that had set her on edge?

She glanced at the back seat where the children were sitting. "I don't see the supplies you bought for Hendrick. I hope we didn't interfere with your errand."

"Everything's in the trunk. I was finished with my shopping when I caught sight of you," he lied.

She was silent as she stared out the window, and when they reached the museum parking lot she gave him a perfunctory thank you.

"I want to ride back with Kyle," Pamela said, and,

without waiting for permission, climbed into the front seat that Ashley had vacated.

"Me, too," said Benny. "Scoot over. There's room for three."

"Well, I guess I've been deserted. Do you mind?" she asked Kyle, secretly relieved to have some time to herself. Not having to referee two tired kids would be a blessing. "I think I can find my way back. I kinda remember how I got here."

"Just follow me. I know a shortcut."

Kyle made sure she was following him and kept her car in his rearview mirror as they took a narrow road that cut across the middle of the island to the row of private homes on the southeasterly beaches.

Ashley knew that there wouldn't be time for the children to rest before dinner. They were tired from the outing and were already squabbling with each other when they got out of Kyle's car.

"That's enough," she said more sharply than she had intended. She saw Kyle raise his eyebrows, but at the moment, she was more afraid of Mrs. Borsch's displeasure than his. He leaned up against his car and watched as she herded the two children into the house.

As they crossed the front foyer, Ashley was relieved that the housekeeper wasn't waiting there with her arms crossed, tapping a black shoe, and with a reprimand on her stiff lips for barely making it back before dinner.

Ashley hurried the children to their rooms with firm

orders to be ready when Lily came to take them to dinner.

She hurried to the nursery. When she saw Lily walking the floor with a fussy baby, she apologized for being late. "I'm sorry. I tried to cram in too many things for one afternoon."

"No matter," Lily said with her usual good nature. She lowered her voice. "I'll take Davie at his worst over Mrs. Borsch at her best."

Ashley chuckled and nodded. "Well, I hope she'll forgive both of us for my tardiness. You'd better scoot now or both of us will be on her black list."

"Cook's in a tizzy. Don't know what's going on, but I'd better have the children fed and out of the way by seven. Mrs. Borsch told me to tell you that you're expected at dinner tonight, and not to plan on having a tray in your room."

And what will she do if I tell her to go fly a kite? Ashley thought, wishing she could act for herself and not her sister. She knew it would be foolish to set up an adversarial relationship with the housekeeper that Jill would have to live with. She'd already created enough antagonism with Hendrick to put her sister in bad with him.

"I'll be back at seven so you can go downstairs," Lily said as she gave the baby to Ashley.

As she took him, Davie cried louder than before. She put him over one shoulder and patted his little back as Lily had been doing, but with no visible effect in soothing him.

"I think he's got a touch of colic," Lily said. "The

poor little thing acts hungry but he doesn't need another bottle. He'll just spit it up if you give him any more milk. Why don't you sit down and lay him across your lap, tummy down?'' she suggested. ''He might like that for a little while, at least.''

With this rather dubious encouragement, Lily hurried out of the room, closing the door behind her. Ashley didn't know how Davie's little lungs could fill the nursery with such loud indignant protests demanding something that she was too stupid to understand.

''It's all right, Davie. Be nice. Be nice,'' she pleaded as she sat down in the rocker and followed Lily's suggestion, gently putting the baby on his tummy across her lap. Whether because of the position of his body, or the comfort it gave him, his cries lost some of their volume. Little by little she could feel the tension in him ease. His cries diminished, and when his eyelids fluttered closed she held her own breath and prayed that he would go to sleep.

Trapped in the rocking chair with the baby drifting off to sleep on her lap, there was nothing she could do but rest her head against the high back of the chair and close her own eyes. The events of the afternoon filled her mind and she tried to sort them out.

She had intended to call Jill as soon as she returned to the room to ask about the loathsome man who seemed to know her. Just remembering his salacious big-toothed smile and the ugly hairy hand he'd held out to her created a shiver between her shoulder blades. Would he have stalked her if Kyle hadn't shown up?

As she sat there, she heard voices out in the hall and recognized Kyle's. The hour they'd spent on the river had shown a side of him that wasn't a part of his persona around the house. He seemed less guarded, or was it less manipulative? *Manipulative?* Why did she use that word? she wondered. From the very beginning she'd felt that he was orchestrating some kind of hidden agenda. His position in the house was vague enough. He seemed to have no responsibility toward the staff. Mrs. Borsch was the controlling hand as far as Ashley could tell. Would an intelligent, capable man like Kyle be content to act as a kind of glorified overseer when there didn't seem to be anything of importance to oversee?

Jill had always teased her about analyzing people when it was much easier to just accept them at face value. Ashley knew that Jill would have no trouble relating to Kyle as a good-looking man who might spice life up a little by flirting with her.

Ashley sighed, looked at her watch, and realized she had less than fifteen minutes to get ready for dinner. As carefully as she could, she lifted the baby up and gingerly carried him over to the crib. As she laid him down, he stirred, moving his head from one side to the other, but his eyes remained closed.

Ashley held her breath for a long moment, but his little arms continued to stretch above his head. His eyes were closed and his little mouth was pursed in contented sleep.

Very quietly she tiptoed out of the nursery. After a quick shower, she changed into a silk peacock-blue jumpsuit. Her wavy hair was still damp and falling in loose ringlets around her face as she fastened in a pair of pearl earrings. She was finishing putting on her makeup—or rather, Jill's usual makeup—when Lily came to relieve her.

"Wow," Lily breathed with open envy as Ashley stood up. "If I had a figure like that, I'd take off for the Big Apple and become a model straight away. You look fabulous."

As she passed the children's rooms, Ashley saw that Pamela was sitting at her desk and Benny was sprawled on his rug, playing with his airplanes. She wished she had time to pop in and see his collection, but she was already ten minutes late getting down-stairs.

The sitting room at the head of the stairs was in shadows, but the screen of a small television set in the far corner was on, and Ashley wondered if the children had forgotten to turn it off. Even as her glance took in the television screen, she heard the soft click of a remote control and the set went dark. Then a figure rose, turned and came toward her.

She saw the big-toothed smile before anything else. A spasm of nausea hit her stomach. No, it couldn't be! The man from the park. Here! In the house. Looming over her with a smile that turned her blood to ice crystals.

"So we meet again, Mrs. Gordon." His voice

sounded as oily and slippery as a serpent slipping through dark foliage. "Shall we go down to dinner?"

Ashley was unable to speak or move. Her mind refused to handle the truth. It was insane to think that this repulsive man was here, under this roof. Rudy Dietz, a guest in the house? There had to be another explanation.

"You look surprised to see me. I was hoping your memory might have improved by now, but I see it hasn't." He spoke in an oily manner that made the contrast between his abrasive looks and his speech even more repulsive. "No matter, we'll have plenty of time to get reacquainted during my stay. I have a room on this floor." His ugly smile broadened.

Ashley took a step backward, appalled at the very idea that he could invade her privacy at will. Only Kyle's quick steps coming up the staircase stopped her from turning her back on the man and retreating to her room.

"Oh, there you are," Kyle said with an impatient edge to his voice. "Hendrick is beginning to growl, so we'd better get ourselves settled for dinner. I see you two have met," he added as if it was the most ordinary of circumstances, but silently he swore. He'd thought he had the situation under control by arranging to introduce Rudy at dinner, but from Ashley's stiff posture and expression of pointed distaste, he could see that he was too late.

Blast it all. He'd warned Hugo that bringing Rudy into the situation could jeopardize everything, but his boss wouldn't listen. The conversation had been a frustrating one for Kyle.

"If you need some heavy arm-twisting with that gal," Hugo had said. "Rudy's your man."

"I'm handling things just fine," Kyle had insisted. "The guest house has only one bedroom, and I don't like the idea of putting Rudy in the house with her."

"Why not? He'll be able to keep a closer eye on our little pigeon."

But, damn it, I'll have to keep a close eye on him, Kyle had sworn silently.

Nothing was going right. It was bad luck that Rudy had shown up that afternoon while he was away keeping an eye on Jill. She was obviously upset by Rudy's presence. Was there some history between them? Is that why she was so upset? Mrs. Borsch had put him in a room just down the hall from Jill and the children. Blast it all! Kyle knew that this arrangement would put all kinds of added pressures on him. Now, he was faced with keeping up a front with Rudy, Hugo's strong arm, as well as making certain the unpredictable Jill Gordon didn't bring everything down on their heads like a deck of cards.

Chapter Seven

"I heard we're having lobster tails," Kyle said brightly, trying to ignore Ashley's rigidity and distant manner. "I don't know about you but I worked up an appetite this afternoon on our little boat ride. Come on, let's go down to dinner before Hendrick gets his back up and serves us bologna sandwiches."

He didn't give her a chance to protest. He took her arm and kept himself between her and Rudy as they made their way to the family dining room. He could tell from her wooden expression that whatever Rudy had said to her had invited a cold shoulder and her determination to ignore him.

Gerta was waiting for them, and she quickly disappeared through the pantry door when they came into the dining room. As Kyle eased Ashley's chair in to the table, her familiar scent triggered the memory of the afternoon's outing and the hours they'd spent together. Tonight her totally feminine figure in the blue jumpsuit created a tantalizing urge to brush a kiss on the softness of her neck as he stood behind her.

Something in his face must have given him away because he saw a twisted curve in Rudy's lips as he watched. "Easy on the eyes, isn't she?"

Heat flared up in Ashley's cheeks. If Kyle hadn't been standing behind her, she might have scooted back her chair and left the room. As if sensing her recoil, he gave her shoulder a light reassuring squeeze, and then moved to her side and asked her if she'd like something from the bar.

"No, thank you," she politely refused.

"Perhaps wine with dinner?"

Something in his tone made her look at him, and his eyes seemed to beg her forgiveness for subjecting her to the man's unpleasant company. At that moment, she sensed that he disliked Rudy as much as she did. This intuitive knowledge brought a warmth of reassurance, but why was the man a guest in the house? And why was Kyle being overtly polite and solicitous to him?

Rudy mixed himself a whiskey and water, and sat down at the table again, just as Gerta returned to serve the first course, tempting bowls of vichyssoise. The taste revived Ashley's appetite, stunted by the presence of the distasteful dinner guest.

During most of the meal, she pointedly ignored the two men as they exchanged some news about mutual acquaintances, basketball games and prospects for Vandenburg's team next season. Jill was undoubtedly knowledgeable about players, teams and national ratings, but Ashley prayed that the two men wouldn't try to draw her into the conversation. The few times a question came her way, she answered it in such vague terms that it put an end to any further discussion.

She gave her attention to the meal. The baked lobster tails were delicious, served with Lyonnaise potatoes and grilled tomatoes with cheese and garlic. Never in her life had she had such wonderful food. There was no doubt that Hendrick was as talented as a master chef, but he was a total failure when it came to handling people.

As the meal progressed, she was thankful that Rudy had not made any more references to any previous meetings. As soon as she got back to her room, she would call Jill and ask about him so she would be prepared if he brought it up again. The meal was nearly over when her luck ran out.

They were finishing a dessert of Dutch apple tart and whipped cream when Rudy leaned back in his chair and surveyed her with a smile that didn't match his piercing dark eyes. "Well, Jill, now that you've had a chance to refresh your memory, you're not going to pretend that you've forgotten the tango we did at the Basketball Hall of Fame dance, are you?"

Startled, Ashley tried for a light laugh that could mean anything, but it sounded horribly phony in her own ears. The delicious lobster dinner suddenly took a sour turn in her stomach. She flashed a quick look at Kyle and was startled to see Kyle's appraising eyes on her as if he were suddenly a stranger waiting to see what her answer was going to be.

Ashley set her coffee cup down, and forced herself to smile at the vulture-like man. *Jill? What would you say and do?* "You really don't expect me to remember every man I've danced with, do you?" she asked lightly.

Rudy's eyes narrowed with a fiery gleam. "You gave me the impression that no one had ever made love to you on the dance floor before."

"Oh, is that what you were doing?" Ashley heard herself saying, and her flippant answer instantly brought an ugly color to his bony cheeks. She didn't know where the retort came from but fright always sharpened her tongue, and deep inside she was frightened of Rudy Dietz. Not only was he offensive to her, but she sensed that he might be sharp enough to detect the charade she was playing. She had the impression that trying to fool him was like handling a lighted stick of dynamite that could go off at any minute.

Kyle lowered his eyes as if fighting back a smile, but the glower on Rudy's face was as threatening as a thundercloud. Before either man could say anything, Ashley quickly pushed back her chair and rose to her feet.

"Please excuse me, I want to get back to the nursery and see how my son is behaving." She didn't wait for their response.

As she left the table, Kyle was painfully conscious of the way the soft, clinging cloth rippled over her tantalizing feminine curves as she moved away. He had had that loveliness in his hands, and he knew how it felt to have the length of her desirable body pressed against his. Jerking his eyes away from her retreating figure, he abruptly got up from his chair and went to the bar to mix another drink.

"She's already gotten to you, hasn't she?" Rudy mocked as he watched Kyle fix his Scotch and water. "She's some broad, all right."

"Don't confuse her with your own brand of women," Kyle answered sharply.

"Well, I'll be damned. Mrs. Borsch was right. She reported to the boss that you were getting all dreamy-eyed around the new nanny. She told him about the fracas with Hendrick, and how you played the hero defending her."

Kyle kept his back to the table while he took a sip of his drink at the bar. *Easy. Easy, don't blow it.* What he did now would determine whether or not Hugo replaced him with Rudy.

As his thoughts raced ahead, he turned around, leaned against the bar, and shrugged. "I'll do what I have to do to get the job done," he said, looking at Rudy over the rim of his glass. "If playing up to Jill Gordon and feeding her vanity will keep her here, then that's what I'll do. But let me give you a warning, Rudy. You try moving in on her, and she'll be out of here quicker than summer lightning."

"Hell, don't be giving me a lecture about how to handle women," Rudy swore. "I don't have to be all nicey-nicey to get the job done. Hugo sent me out here because he thought you might be going soft on the job. From now on, I'm calling the plays.''

Kyle gave him a lazy smile. "I don't think so, Rudy. I have a hell of a lot more chance of keeping our pigeon in the cage than you do. I saw the way she was treating you. Hell, you really must have made a bad impression trying to hustle her on the dance floor. I'll be surprised if she lets you within ten feet of her.''

"Maybe she won't have a choice. The word is out that Budge Gordon's wife and son are here. It shouldn't be too long before we get some action. And if we don't, we may have to force things a little.''

"What do you mean?'' Kyle kept his tone neutral, but the rhythm of his heartbeat suddenly quickened. He didn't want her or the baby put in any more jeopardy than was necessary. Men like Rudy always went for heavy-handed tactics.

Rudy showed his ugly teeth. "There are ways to put pressure on her.''

"You do that, and we'll never be able to keep her long enough to get the job done.''

"There are ways to keep her as long as we want,'' Rudy snapped. "You can play the good guy if you want, but when push comes to shove, she's not leaving here until Vandenburg says she can.''

UPSTAIRS, Ashley shut and locked both doors as soon as Lily had gone. With Rudy Dietz in a room just down the hall, she wasn't taking the chance of any casual, pop-in visits. The baby was still asleep, and Ashley lost no time in calling her sister.

As before, she gave the arranged message on the answering machine, hung up and called again.

"Hi, sis," her twin answered. Jill still sounded a little hoarse, but her voice was stronger than before, and there was a lift to her tone that hadn't been there before. "How ya doing?"

"The question is, how are you doing?"

"My cough's about gone. Just a couple of more days and we can make the switch."

Ashley took a deep breath. "Jill, I really think you ought to reconsider taking this job."

There was a moment of silence at Jill's end, then she said sharply, "What? You didn't blow it for me, did you?".

"No, but—"

"That's a relief. I'm feeling a lot better. I should be able to lick this bug enough to take over by the end of the week. You'll have to get away and take the ferry across to the mainland, and I'll meet you there."

"Jill, listen to me. I don't have a good feeling about this place. I really think it would be better for you to find something else."

"Oh, really?" There was a sarcastic edge to Jill's voice. "And what would you suggest I do since I don't have any marketable skills? I'm not exactly in the driver's seat, you know, when it comes to handling the responsibilities of a baby and trying to put a roof over our heads and food on the table. This nanny job may not seem like anything to you, but it's a godsend to me. Of course, you don't have to worry, being a college professor and all that.''

Ashley swallowed back the retort that Jill could have made the same choices about getting an education and supporting herself. ''This isn't about me. It's about what's best for you and Davie.''

''Are you bailing out on me?'' Jill demanded. ''Is that it?''

''No, that's not what I'm talking about.''

''Then what are you talking about? What's wrong with the job?''

For a minute, Ashley had trouble answering. There was nothing wrong with the job, per se. Pamela and Benny were nice kids. They were adaptable to whatever was going on, and Ashley knew that Jill wouldn't have any trouble winning them over. How could she explain the nebulous, dark undercurrent that seemed to permeate the very walls of the house? Maybe her sense of guilt was creating some of the tension, but one thing was not her imagination—Rudy Dietz, and the evil that fouled the air with his presence.

''Do you know a Rudy Dietz?''

''I know who he is. I mean, he was always hanging around Budge's basketball team. I think the guy works for Hugo. Why?''

''He's here at the house. At dinner tonight, he claimed to have made love to you on the dance floor.''

Jill laughed. ''Well, I don't remember that, but

Budge and I used to go to some swinging parties. I danced with a lot of fellows, and sometimes things threatened to get a little heavy. But Budge always rescued me when I had too much to drink. Just hold the guy off until I get there, and I'll handle him.''

"He gives me the creeps.''

"Is that what this is all about?'' Jill chided. "You can't handle some guy making a pass at you? What about that handsome hunk you were telling me about? Have you been giving him the freeze, too?''

"No, we have a nice working relationship,'' she said as evenly as she could. "He's really been a help with Benny and Pamela.'' Ashley knew she should tell Jill about what had happened in the pool, and about the companionship she and Kyle had shared on the afternoon's boat excursion, but she needed to sort out her own feelings about Kyle before she shared them with her sister.

Jill asked about Davie, and Ashley assured her that her son was in good hands. "Lily is wonderful with him. You won't need to worry about leaving the baby with her. And you'll enjoy Pamela and Benny, too.''

"Then what's the problem, Ashley? The baby's content, and being a nanny is something I can handle. I really don't understand why you are advising me to chuck the whole thing. Remember, I'm not you. I can roll with the tide, and I don't want you to sink this ship for me before I get there. Just hang loose.''

"I'll try,'' Ashley promised, but she hung up with the feeling that even two or three more days in the deception was going to seem like an eternity.

THE NEXT TWO DAYS with the children went well, and Ashley avoided contact with the men at lunch by having Lily bring her a tray. She guarded against meeting Rudy as she came and went from her room and the nursery, but she didn't see him again in the sitting room or hall. He was absent from the house the second night, and Ashley began to relax, even enjoying dinner with Kyle as if he, too, were relieved not to have the obtrusive man around.

Ashley had some unexpected free time the next afternoon when Joseph offered to take Pamela and Benny fishing with him. Ashley was surprised at the offer because the man seemed too reserved and cold to enjoy spending any time with two kids. Kyle gave his approval, and Mrs. Borsch assured her that they were safe enough with her husband.

"I guess I forgot to tell you that you are to have one afternoon off," she said briskly as if the information really wasn't that important.

"I guess you did," Ashley answered, holding back her temper.

Right after lunch, Ashley saw the fishing party off from the boathouse on the beach. Taking a deep breath, she looked up and down the smooth stretch of private beach, trying to decide what to do with her free hours. She certainly wasn't going to return to the house any sooner than she had to. She felt like an escapee from a self-imposed imprisonment. This would probably be the last chance she'd have for exploring Roble Island by herself before she left.

She headed down the beach in a southwesterly direction, and didn't realize how far she'd gone until she caught sight of the top of the old lighthouse in the distance. She remembered that it stood at the tip of the island, and recalled how intriguing the old structure had looked from the excursion boat. She didn't know how far away it was, but she decided that she could always turn back if she got tired.

As the strip of sandy beach began to narrow, shelves of rocks reached out into the water, blocking her path. Watching her footing on glistening old stones that must have been there since the island was formed, she carefully made her way forward around the tip of island.

And suddenly she was there.

Laughing, she hurried forward, reaching the sheltered cove where the old lighthouse stood in a tangle of vines and shrubs. Like the tattered garb of an old queen, the rusty iron cupola and darkened windows still stood proudly against the blue-white sky. Once yellow lights had beamed out across this open entrance to the sea and as always, the enchantment of a time gone by touched Ashley with a quickening of breath.

She could fantasize schooners, pirate ships and men-of-war plying the waters on a darkened night around that warning beam of guiding light. For a moment, she entertained a sense of regret that she wouldn't be able to share this experience with Benny and Pamela. Maybe Jill would read some sailor stories and bring them here.

As she climbed up to the lighthouse and circled its

base, she was grateful for her jeans and walking shoes. There wasn't much to see on the outside of the old structure, but someone had broken the lock on the lower door and it stood slightly ajar. She couldn't resist the temptation to open it wider and peek inside.

KYLE HAD BEEN TRYING to keep her in sight as he stayed his distance behind her. He didn't want her to glance back and see him following her as he pushed through the thick undergrowth of myrtle bushes and palmettos above the white beach. Arranging for Joseph to take the kids for an afternoon had given her a chance to be on her own. He was gambling that she was about to make some kind of move. Maybe Budge had contacted her. Or maybe she was the one who had called him—maybe the other afternoon from the museum. A lot depended upon her ignorance of the constant surveillance she was under. He didn't like the idea of Rudy taking the night shift, watching Jill's bedroom door, just waiting for her to try and give him the slip, but there was little Kyle could do about it. It worried him that Hugo had decided he couldn't handle things by himself.

Now he had two flanks to watch.

Kyle increased his pace and had just reached the edge of the cove when he heard a faint cry. He bolted forward. As his searching eyes swept the small inlet, he half expected to see a boat or someone else there.

The cove was empty.

She wasn't anywhere in sight, and the silence was only broken by the cries of seagulls at the water's edge. What was the sound he had heard? Had she been calling to someone? His instinct was to shout her name, but experience had taught him to be cautious. He didn't know what might be going down, and acting like a charging bull could put both of them in jeopardy.

There was no sign of movement around the lighthouse. Moving as quietly as he could, he mounted the rocky ground, and when he reached the weathered base, he carefully eased his way around it.

At the same time as he saw the half-open door, he heard sounds inside. Pressing up against the wall, he waited. If she had arranged to meet someone here, he needed the element of surprise to get the upper hand. He didn't want to move too soon. He had to be sure that—

The rest of the thought was lost when a muffled cry of pain jerked him into action. He kicked the door all the way open and charged into the darkened room.

Ashley couldn't tell who loomed over her in the shadowy darkness until the light from the door silhouetted his figure. "Kyle?" she gasped.

He was so certain that someone had been with her that it took him a long minute to realize he'd been mistaken. His gaze darted around the rounded room. The place was empty, and the stairway had been removed.

"Be careful where you step," she warned him. He realized then that she was sitting on the floor trying to pull her leg out of some splintered floor boards. "I fell through."

"What in the hell were you doing in here, anyway?" he demanded as he bent down beside her.

"I just thought I'd take a peek around and...." Her voice trailed off into tears of frustration.

"Don't move." He could feel the boards sagging under his own weight. They'd be damn lucky if the whole floor didn't give way.

"I tried pulling my leg out, but it just hurts and won't come. I think it's caught between two splintered boards, but I can't really see. It's so dark in here."

As he let his hands slide along the floor, he discovered that it was only one board that had broken and trapped her leg between the two split pieces. He just prayed he could make a bigger hole without weakening the surrounding planks.

"All right, let's get you out of here," he said with false confidence. One side of the splintered board would have to be broken off in order to free her leg. He didn't dare think about the whole floor giving way and burying them in a heap of rotten wood.

"What are you going to do?" she asked as he stood up.

"I'm going to try and break off the piece of wood that's trapped your leg." He stood beside her and rested his hand on her shoulder. Giving her a reassuring squeeze, he raised a foot and brought it down as hard as he could on one end of the jagged board.

The sharp crackle of dry wood stabbed their ears as clouds of dust rising from the vibration of the floorboards filled their nostrils and burned their eyes.

Coughing, Kyle brushed a hand across his eyes just as Ashley gave a triumphant yell. "You did it. I'm free."

His arms went around her and he helped her stand. "Let's get the hell out of here."

As fast as he could, he hurriedly guided her across the creaking boards and out into the blessed sunshine.

She let out a soft whimper and he pulled her in close. "It's okay. You're all right now."

As she trembled, he ran soothing fingers down her back, and she felt his warm breath on her cheek. Secure in his arms, she was strangely detached from the pain in her leg. For a long moment they stood there, clinging to each other.

Kyle knew the danger that this kind of temptation invited, and he also knew with frightening certainty that somehow he was about to lose a firm rein on his emotions. He would have laughed if someone had told him he could feel this way about any woman...especially one he'd have sworn on a stack of Bibles could never tempt him.

Chapter Eight

As Kyle pulled away from her, Ashley knew from the hard tilt of his chin, brown eyes that were guarded and distant, and the firm set of his mouth that he was angry with her. And no wonder, she thought contritely. She'd put them both in danger with her insatiable curiosity. If he hadn't come along— Her thinking screeched to a stop.

"How did you know where I was?" she asked with a questioning lift of an eyebrow.

"I followed you," he answered honestly. The truth was always the best policy, even if it had to be modified. "I came down to the dock too late to see the kids off, but I saw you walking a distance down the beach and decided to catch up with you." He managed a wry smile. "I didn't know you were leading me into a rescue mission."

"Oh. Well, I'm grateful that you showed up."

"Me, too," he agreed. Silently he wondered why she'd made for the lighthouse in the first place. He was pretty sure she hadn't had time to meet up with anyone, either in the cove or the lighthouse. He was puzzled. Had an arranged rendezvous been thwarted for some reason?

Ashley groaned as she stuck her scraped leg out in front of her. The pant leg was torn, and blood had soaked the cloth. The scratch on her upper thigh was superficial, but it burned like a dozen cigarettes pressed into her skin.

"We'd better wash your leg and see if there are any splinters embedded in the skin. Come on, there's an artesian spring not far from here. Some nice cool water will make it feel better. Can you walk all right?"

"Of course. It's just a scratch," she said defensively. She felt enough of a fool without him treating her as an invalid.

"You were lucky," he said shortly and took her hand firmly in his.

She knew it would be childish to pull away; besides, she was more shaken than she'd ever admit. Even now, the terror of being trapped sent a cold chill trickling down her spine.

Neither of them spoke as they made their way away from the cove and the beach, heading into a wild entanglement of trees and thick undergrowth. She would never have dared to try and find her way back to the house this way. It must be shorter than following the ocean's edge, but she couldn't even see a path through the forest of trees, wild azaleas, jasmine vines and myrtle bushes.

She was grateful for his hand as he led the way.

She marveled at the riot of brilliantly colored flowers and patches of deep green grass shaded by overhanging trees. A quiet enchantment surrounded them, broken only by the soft tread of their footsteps and the fluttering of birds overhead.

He seemed to know exactly where the clear waters of an artesian spring had created a small pond that shimmered gold-green in the dappled sunlight filtering through a canopy of branches.

"It's beautiful," she murmured as she looked around. "How did you ever find it?" she asked, forgetting for a moment the smarting rawness in her leg as she eased down on the grassy bank edging the water.

"Just lucky, I guess," he answered vaguely. He wondered why he had been so willing to bring her here and share his private retreat with her. There were plenty of other freshwater creeks and springs in the area, and any one of them would have served the purpose of cleaning her wound. There had been no need to bring her to his special place.

As he stood there, looking down at her, he knew with sudden clarity this secret retreat would never be the same. In spite of himself, he would always see her sitting there in the jeweled grass, her honey-gold hair caught in a radiance of filtered sunlight and her lovely eyes taking in the beauty around her. How could he ever forget the supple grace of her body as she leaned forward to cup the clear spring water in her hands? A lovely nymph in an enchanted setting.

"Oh, it's cold," she said with childish delight.

As he eased down beside her, her outward innocence only inflamed his desire, and he was sure that she was perfectly aware of the yearning she was creating in him. He was angry with himself for responding to it and said gruffly, "Why don't you tear off a piece of that torn pant leg and use it as a rag to clean your leg? Unless you want to strip down and take a fresh-water dip right here and now?"

"Skinny dipping isn't my thing," she answered evenly, her smile fading.

"Too bad," he said in a flippant tone that he hoped disguised his own distaste for the crudeness. He certainly didn't want her to know how successful she was at stirring his emotions. When Hugo had set up this baited trap and put him in charge, Kyle had viewed it as strictly business, but Jill Gordon was becoming much more to him than a pawn in a dangerous game. It didn't help to know she was married to a man who didn't deserve her.

"I told you I was sorry," she said, following his suggestion and tearing a piece of denim from the ripped pant leg. "There's no need to make me feel any worse than I already do." She gave her attention to her leg, relieved that it wasn't a deep scratch and would soon heal.

"Just what were you up to?" he asked bluntly, deciding he'd quit shadowboxing.

"I wasn't *up* to anything. I'm intrigued by old landmarks like lighthouses."

"Really? Why the fascination?" Getting her to reveal herself could only make his job easier. He had to admit she'd handed him more surprises than he had expected.

"I like history," she said simply.

"Well, there's plenty of history on this old island."

"I know. I've been doing some reading in the library. This very spring could have been used by Indians and African slaves at the same time the Spanish and English were settling on the island. Imagine it!" For a moment, she forgot herself, and in the hushed silence she could almost hear soft footsteps coming through the thick undergrowth as the first settlers came to fill vessels of clear, cold water.

Kyle saw her eyes suddenly glow with wonder and realized that she was telling the truth. She wasn't pretending at all. Deliberately, he began to ply her with questions, and was astounded at the wealth of historical knowledge that she had already picked up about the island. "You surprise me, Jill," he said honestly.

Too late, Ashley realized that she'd revealed a lot more of herself than she'd intended. Her natural gift for researching the past had spilled out as she'd talked about the things she'd learned about the island's history. The emotional stress of the incident in the lighthouse had made her careless.

Kyle listened to her, trying to reconcile this intellectually sharp beauty with what he'd been told about Budge Gordon's wife. Maybe Hugo had been certain that they could manipulate her for their own purposes, but Kyle wasn't so sure. Some intuitive sense warned him that Jill may be holding a trump card that he didn't know about.

She drew in fragrant perfume from nearby flowers and water lilies dotting the water, and he leaned back on his arms, letting his gaze trace the slivers of sunlight and shadows playing on leaves and grass. As they sat there, the only sound the trickle of water moving into the pond, there seemed to be no need for any more words. It was a rare experience for him, this silent communication with a woman that he was committed to betraying.

Ashley knew that these were moments that she would take with her like a hidden treasure, to be taken out and renewed when she had returned to her own life. Time had no relevance until she finally said reluctantly, "We'd better be getting back."

Kyle nodded, eased to his feet and held out his hand to steady her as she got up. If she had looked up at him, he would have been lost. Never had he wanted to make love to a woman as much as he did at that moment, but her distant manner and rigid body stopped him. Whatever had been happening between them was gone, and a surge of regret replaced the desire that had been racing through his veins.

When they returned to the house, as luck would have it, the first person they ran into was Rudy. The abrasive man was standing on the back terrace, watching them as they came up the path. His glistening eyes took in Ashley's disheveled appearance, traveling from her tousled hair down to her torn pants. A knowing smirk made her feel dirty all over.

"Let me guess. You've been enjoying a romp in the woods?"

"Save it, Rudy," Kyle snapped, well aware that his clothes were dusty from the ordeal in the lighthouse and there were green stains on his pants where he'd sat on the grassy bank. "Jill had a little accident. We need to get some antiseptic on her leg."

Rudy's eyes narrowed as he saw the bloody scrape on Jill's bare thigh. "What happened?"

"Later, Rudy," Kyle said with a warning in his tone. He guided Ashley past Rudy and through a terrace door into the house. "Go on up to your room, and I'll be up with a first aid kit—"

"Don't bother," Ashley told him shortly, smarting from the embarrassment of the whole situation. "There's one in the nursery."

Without looking back at him, she hurried down the hall, and up the stairs to her bedroom. Just imagining what the two men were saying about her sent a hot flush of embarrassment through her.

She felt like such a fool, and Jill would be furious with her. As soon as she cleaned up and Lily was gone, she'd have to call her sister and try to explain why Jill would have to wear long shirts or slacks for a while to hide the absence of scratches.

HER TWIN EXPLODED as Ashley knew she would when told about the incident.

"You did *what?*"

"I know it sounds foolish now, but it seemed like a rare chance for me to visit a vintage lighthouse. I should have paid attention to the broken lock on the door, but I didn't. Anyway, one of the floorboards broke and I scraped my leg. Kyle came along and got me free. I'll write down all the details.''

"I can't believe you'd do such a stupid thing, Ashley. Now I won't get to enjoy the beach or wear any of my miniskirts.''

"It's not a deep scratch—"

"What if you'd broken your leg, what then? I have to break mine?''

"Don't be childish, Jill," Ashley answered sharply. "You'd better be damn glad I'm trying to hold this stupid job for you. I'm ready to leave now. Just say the word and I'm out of here. I don't know why I let you talk me into this in the first place.''

Jill instantly changed her tune. "I do appreciate what you're doing, sis. I really do. It's just that I'm tired out from fighting this bug and worrying. I'll spend tomorrow getting ready, and meet you the following afternoon. Call me tomorrow night and we'll make arrangements, okay?''

"Fine." Ashley took a deep breath. "I don't suppose I can talk you out of taking this job?''

"Nope. I don't have any other options. Besides, I'm looking forward to meeting the Pierce Brosnan look-alike. You didn't set up the damsel-in-distress scenario on purpose, did you?'' Jill chuckled. "Maybe I ought to thank you for putting us on such an intimate base.''

"Sorry to disappoint you. Kyle's outward congeniality is carefully measured, and, apparently, he's very careful not to get intimate with anyone.''

"You sound a little edgy. Has this guy gotten to you—or me, as the case may be?"

"Of course not."

"No casual flirtation or anything?"

"No, but his attentiveness seems almost manipulative. I'll be interested to hear your take on him."

"Well, I won't be digging beneath the surface the way you do. Really, sis, you're never going to have any romance in your life if you're always trying to dissect every man you meet."

After Ashley hung up, she thought about what Jill had said. Was she trying to dissect Kyle Stone, or just understand him?

ASHLEY HAD a dinner tray in her room that evening. She just couldn't bring herself to go down and face the men and Gerta. She didn't know what explanation Kyle had given Rudy, but the horrid man would, undoubtedly, relish embarrassing her at the first opportunity. Jill would probably be able to give him as good as he gave, and Ashley was glad that she only had one more full day to put up with his presence.

She played with Davie, and listened to Benny's and Pamela's excited account of their fishing trip. The children sat on the bed beside her and Davie. Both of them were flushed with reddish tans from a day of sun and water. They were chattering happily, and she had a moment of regret that her challenge as a nanny was almost over. In a few days she would be back in her small Colorado apartment, shut off from any kind of contact with them.

Jill had never been one to keep in close touch—unless she needed something. Ashley doubted that she would hear anything about life on Roble Island once she left it.

KYLE LISTENED to the raging tropical storm that had blown in and kept one ear tuned to the radio, relieved that they were predicting it to be a fast-moving storm drenching Florida, Georgia and the eastern seaboard. By tomorrow afternoon, things should be drying out, and the sun would be back again.

Feeling at odds with himself, he dropped down into an easy chair in the small living room, and, leaning his head back, he shifted through the events of the day, and what they might mean in the long run.

He was surprised when he heard a sharp knocking on his door, and he sprang up quickly. For some nebulous reason, or wishful thinking, he was half expecting to see Ashley there, but when he threw open the door, it was Rudy in a black slicker and wide-brimmed rain hat.

Kyle silently cursed. Dinner had been a contest of wills. Rudy had accused Kyle of losing his perspective, and it was clear that he was determined to take charge. Kyle was just as determined that the violent man wasn't going to start running things. The confrontation had ended in an impasse. Kyle was irritated that here he was again, ready to try and throw his weight around.

''What in blazes are you doing out in this storm?'' Kyle swore.

"We need to talk," Rudy said with that ugly smile as he flung water all over the rug getting out of his hat and rain slicker.

"Couldn't it wait until morning?"

"Hell, no. You think I'd get out in this storm if it wasn't important?"

Kyle could tell from the gleam in Rudy's dark eyes that he was pleased about something. Kyle felt a sudden tightening in his chest. "All right. What is it, Rudy?"

"Fix me a drink and I'll tell you. A brandy nightcap goes good on a night like this, don't you think?"

Kyle swore under his breath and crossed the room to a small bar set into one wall. He knew that he had no choice but to play along. He felt as if Rudy had him dangling from a string and was holding a big pair of shears ready to cut him loose. One thing was sure, Rudy wasn't going to do any talking until he was ready, and Kyle couldn't afford to dismiss anything he had to say.

Kyle turned off the radio, fixed them each a snifter of brandy and handed one to Rudy who was sitting on the sofa, his long legs stuck out in front of him.

Easing down into a soft chair, Kyle acted as if he had all the time in the world to hear what Rudy had to say. He was determined not to show any undue interest in his guest's visit. As they sipped their drinks, the only sound was wind and rain slashing the small house as if trying to sweep it down to the rolling sea where huge breakers were pounding the beach.

"Some storm," Rudy said idly, his eyes almost gloating as they met Kyle's over the rim of his glass.

Kyle nodded. How to play a waiting game was something he'd learned a long time ago. He wasn't about to reveal any undue interest in what was making Rudy look almost gleeful. Kyle knew the man wouldn't be able to contain himself for long.

He was right.

After a couple more sips of brandy, Rudy said casually, "I called Hugo tonight. We had a nice little conversation. I thought he ought to know what's going on around here."

Kyle swallowed back a flare of anger as he said evenly, "I suppose you fed him a lot of half truths and innuendoes. There's nothing to report, and you know it, Rudy. Getting the boss all riled up isn't going to help matters. Now I'll have to call him and set him straight."

"Oh, you don't have to call him," Rudy said smugly. "You can tell him yourself. He's coming down from New York in a couple of days. I guess he wants to check on the situation himself."

Damn it. Leave it to Rudy to foul up everything.

"Maybe when I tell him the true situation, he'll change his mind," Kyle snapped.

"I don't think he trusts you, Kyle, especially where women are concerned. Didn't you get into something sticky where a go-go dancer was concerned? I guess some women just can't resist that boyish charm of yours. What a curse to be so damn good-looking," he taunted. "I told Hugo that it might be better for me to handle this job alone."

Kyle managed a sarcastic laugh. "I'll bet you did, Rudy, but when he sees how Jill Gordon gives you a wide berth, he'll probably put you on another job pronto. Maybe it's a good thing the boss is coming to evaluate the situation. I don't know what you told him about your past acquaintance with Jill, but it's obvious she can't stand to be around you. I don't think he'll take a chance on the fact that she might leave because she abhors the sight of you."

"We'll let Hugo decide," Rudy snapped. "When he sees how the two of you are carrying on, he'll trust me to do what has to be done when the time comes. You've gone soft on her! Anyone with one eye in his head can see that."

"I know my job."

"Like hell. You're on your way out, buddy!" Rudy set down his glass with a bang. Then he got to his feet, flung on his hat and slicker, and strode out the door, leaving it wide open so that the fury of the rain and wind whipped into the living room.

Chapter Nine

The sky was overcast the next morning, and the air hung heavy with moisture. The garden was water-logged from the continuing drizzle, but the winds driving the storm had died down. Ashley knew there would be no outside activity for her or the children that afternoon.

The only bright thing in the dreary morning was Davie's happy mood. He gurgled and kicked his legs with joyful abandonment as she bathed him. She nuzzled the sweet-smelling baby and then dressed him in a miniature sailor's romper suit. Gently brushing the yellow fuzz on his head, she decided he was going to have the same natural curl as his mother and aunt. As he nestled in her arms, taking his bottle, she was aware of a tug on her emotions caused by the realization that tomorrow morning would probably be the last day that she would "play mommy." She'd never expected any maternal instinct to be aroused by just caring for Jill's baby for a few days, but on some foolish level, she wished he was hers. Sighing, she quickly shoved the thought away before it could take root.

Her thoughts sped ahead to the arrangements that she and Jill would have to make when she called her that evening. The best time to slip away would be between eleven-thirty in the morning when the children went to lunch and three o'clock in the afternoon when the children's activity time began. She could leave the house on pretense of having lunch in the village, and taking Davie for an outing. She'd catch the twelve o'clock ferry to the mainland where she'd arrange to meet Jill in a rented car. They would change clothes, identification and cars, and Jill could return on the two o'clock ferry. She'd be able to get back to the house before three o'clock and if she were a little late, it wouldn't matter. She could always use the excuse of losing her way, even though Ashley had drawn a map for her and also a blueprint of the house. It wouldn't do to have Jill fumbling around for her room or the nursery. The timetable seemed workable, and, knowing Jill, she'd be able to weasel her way out of any unexpected challenges.

And I'll be free to go back home.

Ashley was surprised at the emptiness that thought created in her. And somewhere in the hollow feeling was the realization that she would probably never see Kyle Stone again. Not that it mattered, she told herself, but an inner voice mocked her attempt to deny that he had engaged her romantic fantasies. If the truth were known, she resented not being able to relate to him as herself. She suspected that Jill would break through the reserve that he carefully maintained, and they would become friends in short order. He might wonder why things had imperceptibly changed between them, but Ashley knew her sister would be able to handle the situation. No doubt she'd have the whole household eating out of her hand.

Ashley sighed, placed a kiss on the sleeping baby's head and laid him gently in his crib. For a moment, as she stood there looking down at him, foolish tears that had no rhyme or reason threatened to spill from the corners of her eyes. Maybe Jill had not chosen wisely in marrying Budge Gordon, but for the first time, Ashley wondered if she were the one, and not Jill, who had missed out on the important things. Suddenly her college degrees and financial independence seemed a poor exchange for love and a family.

Giving her eyes a quick swipe, she went into her bedroom to get ready for the day. She chose soft white slacks that didn't irritate her scratched leg, and a short-sleeved clinging sweater in shades of blue and lavender. Tying back her hair with a matching paisley scarf, she touched pink gloss to her lips and put a hint of blush on her cheeks.

When she'd finished, she viewed herself in the mirror with a satisfied smile. Maybe her sister was right. Wearing a variety of colors instead of bland shades and styles made being a woman a lot more interesting. *Perhaps I'll loosen up and go shopping when I get back to Colorado, and change my wardrobe's color scheme,* she told herself in an effort to lift her heavy mood.

When Lily came in to relieve her, the maid was concerned about Ashley's leg. "Are you sure it's not infected or anything?"

"I'm sure. It's really just a scratch and a small bandage covers it fine."

"You were lucky that Mr. Stone went along with you to see the lighthouse. Just think what might have happened if you'd been alone."

Ashley nodded. So he'd lied and said they'd been on the outing together. What other lies had he told? Just as she'd feared, the whole staff must be humming about the two of them going off together.

As she descended the staircase to the lower floor, the house seemed to be as gray and dank as the weather outside. Her steps sounded hollow on the marble floors as she went down the center hall, and muted light lent a dull pewter patina to the walls and furnishings.

Benny and Pamela were already in the library, and greeted her excitedly. They both had a story that they wanted to dictate to her about yesterday's fishing trip. She was relieved and pleased that Benny and Pamela were enthusiastic about creating their own books and stories. Jill should be able to follow through with the book-writing activity until they tired of it, and then it would be up to her to decide what to do next.

Kyle seemed preoccupied when he came into the library just as they were finishing. She could tell he was only feigning interest in the children's stories. He made all the right responses, but his eyes kept darting to hers as if he had something else on his mind.

As soon as he'd satisfied Pamela and Benny about the merits of their writing skills, he gave them a smile that didn't meet his eyes. "I have some good news."

His voice was cheery enough, but he didn't look like someone dispensing good news. What was the matter?

"Guess who's coming to see you for a few days?"

Benny shot a quick glance at his sister. Ashley could feel the sudden tension in their stiff little bodies.

The little girl visibly swallowed. "Grandfather?"

Kyle nodded. "Yes, your grandfather. He'll be here sometime tomorrow."

Ashley's stomach took a sickening plunge. No, not tomorrow. Hugo knew Jill! They would have to make the switch before he got here. Afraid that her expression was as revealing as the children's, she turned away quickly and pretended to be straightening up the morning's work.

"He's bringing some guests with him. There's going to be party," Kyle said, obviously trying to put a good light on their grandfather's visit. "Hendrick and Mrs. Borsch are already busy making plans. Maybe you'll know some of the people and be glad to see them again."

"No, we won't," Benny said belligerently with a scowl.

"We don't like Grandfather's friends," Pamela said with a grown-up solemnity and childlike honesty.

"Well, I bet they're going to like you and your new nanny," he said brightly.

She knew he was looking at her, but she kept her eyes lowered as she handled papers on the desk, hoping that he wouldn't notice the slight trembling of her fingers as her frantic thoughts flew in every direction. She had to leave before Hugo showed up. Not only did he know Jill, but it was a good bet that the people he was bringing with him also knew her. A prickling of fear sent a chill through her as she thought about the narrow window of time that they had in which to make the switch.

Kyle had expected the children's negative reaction. They'd never pretended to like the autocratic grandfather who ran the family and who told everyone what they could or could not do. He knew the children's parents were under Hugo's thumb as well, and were afraid to go against his wishes.

It was Jill Gordon's response that surprised him. Obviously, she wasn't any more enthusiastic about Hugo's visit than his grandchildren. Instead of reassuring Benny and Pamela that their grandfather would be pleased with their creative work, she was strangely silent.

Kyle worried now that she might suddenly up and leave. He silently swore at Rudy for throwing everything off balance by convincing Hugo to come and take charge.

"Well, lunch is waiting," he told Benny and Pamela. "You two run on, and we'll join you in a minute." He laughed as they bounded out of the room like two puppies set free from their leashes.

"Kids," he said shaking his head as he walked

over to the desk where she was still gathering up the morning's work. "Don't you wish sometimes that adults could be that spontaneous?"

"Yes," she said, pulling at her lip. What should she do now?

He stood close enough to smell the lemony freshness of her soft hair, and see the faint trace of a tan on her nose and cheeks. A soft knitted sweater molded the full curves of her breasts and hugged her narrow waistline. His hands wanted to slip around her waist and draw her against him.

"You're doing a fantastic job with the kids," he said, wondering why she was so stiff and aloof with him.

"Thank you."

"How's the leg?"

"Fine."

"You know what the word *fine* stands for, don't you? Feelings Inside Not Expressed."

She took a deep breath and turned around. "In this case, fine means fine, really. Another day or two and the scratch will be completely gone."

"Glad to hear it."

As she looked up at him, he noticed that the paisley scarf brought out the lavender hue in her liquid blue eyes. But he also saw in their depths a darkening that matched the tight corners of her lips.

Something was wrong. Had Rudy been at her again? Kyle's hands tightened as if he had the man's scrawny neck in his grasp. He knew then that he had become her protector even at the cost of more danger to himself.

LUNCH WAS a quiet affair. Kyle left the table early, excusing himself to take care of some matters before his boss arrived. ''He's planning on arriving in time for dinner tomorrow evening.''

Ashley's stomach took a sickening dip. There wasn't going to be much leeway in getting Jill in place before Hugo arrived.

Everything would have to go like clockwork.

When she and the children left the family dining room, they were engulfed in a harried bustle that resounded throughout the house. Additional staff had arrived, and Mrs. Borsch was like a commander-in-chief giving orders to the new troops.

Double doors on the main floor had been flung open, and draped furniture was being uncovered. There was a scurry of cleaning and polishing, and vast floral displays were appearing all over the house.

As Ashley peeked into rooms that had been shut, she was astounded at the beautiful decorative ceilings, carved woodwork and furnishings that were an antique-lover's dream.

''What are we going to do this afternoon?'' Pamela asked as she glanced out a window at the sodden landscape.

''We're going to take a field trip,'' Ashley answered with sudden inspiration, deciding to shift the time of the afternoon activity to right now.

''A field trip? Where?'' Pamela frowned.

"Around the house."

Benny groaned. "What a bummer."

"Your grandfather has collected a lot of wonderful things that you need to appreciate. You're very lucky to have a museum right here under your very own roof."

"I'd rather go swimming, Jilly."

She chuckled at Benny's frankness. "All right. We'll spend an hour going through the house and an hour swimming. Deal?"

"Deal," he said with a lopsided grin.

Ashley knew that she had proposed the tour as much for herself as the children. This would be her last chance to see Hugo's collection of paintings, furniture and art objects. She knew that Jill would have little interest in such treasures, and Ashley cautioned herself not to show too much enthusiasm or knowledge as they walked through the rooms.

Ashley hadn't realized how much of the house had been shut off. When they walked into a spacious dining room with an arched ceiling and gold-leaf-framed bevelled mirrors, she could visualize the glitter of a dozen guests sitting under the pair of crystal chandeliers hanging over the long table. Two enormous sideboards were beautifully engraved with renaissance designs. Gerta and another woman were already busy getting the room in order, but Ashley ignored their frowns as she pointed out intricate patterns in the cherrywood pieces.

She and the children spent nearly an hour in the hall, viewing marble statuary and wall hangings.

When they went into the main living room, Ashley saw with surprise that most of the furniture was quite modern, undoubtedly purchased from the most expensive furniture makers in America and abroad.

In one corner, a glass cabinet held a marvelous collection of snuff boxes and ornate figurines. Ashley couldn't begin to estimate their value, but she knew that the original oil paintings hanging on the wall were worth thousands of dollars.

She was so engrossed in explaining how the oil paintings differed in painting technique from a collection of watercolors on an adjoining wall that she wasn't aware Kyle had joined them until she heard Pamela say, "We're on a field trip, Kyle. You want to come?"

Ashley flushed with sudden heat in her cheeks. He must think her a total fool.

"Sure, why not?" Kyle answered smoothly. Mrs. Borsch had come to him a few minutes earlier, ready to explode. The housekeeper's face was an angry ruddy hue as she spat, "She's at it again. You've got to do something before it's too late."

"Too late for what? I don't know what you're talking about," Kyle had answered, mentally stiffening. *What in blazes has gone wrong now?*

"That woman! She's going all over the house, looking at everything. Just like the night she was after the silver. No telling what she's picked up already. You know how Mr. Vandenburg is about his things. If any one little thing is missing, we'll all get the sack."

"Simmer down, Mrs. Borsch," Kyle soothed. "Quit your worrying."

The housekeeper jabbed a bony finger at him. "I knew she was a thief. Knew it the minute I laid eyes on her. She's the one who drove her husband to steal that money, if you ask me. Planned the whole thing or I miss my guess."

"Whoa, slow down, Mrs. Borsch. Let me check it out before you pop a gasket. I'm sure you've jumped to the wrong conclusion," he said with as much conviction as he could. Here we go again, he thought, as he headed to the elegant living room to take care of the situation. Jill Gordon was always putting him off balance. Just when he thought he had her figured out, she'd do something to knock the props out from under him.

He could tell from Jill's expression now that she was totally engrossed in viewing Hugo's expensive art collection.

"You didn't tell me you were an artist," he said with an easy smile. Surely she wasn't looking over the collection with an eye to stealing one?

"I've done a little dabbling," Ashley admitted and started to tell him that the few art classes she'd taken had only made her appreciate great artists even more, then she remembered. Jill had never taken an art course in her life. Suddenly she realized that indulging in her own passion for art and antiques was setting Jill up for some problems.

"Well, I guess that's enough for today," she said quickly. She turned to Benny and Pamela. "You two run along and get your swimming suits. I'll meet you at the pool.''

Ashley sighed as Benny and Pamela left the beautiful living room with the same air of release as her students left the lecture hall at college. "I guess the field trip wasn't such a good idea, after all. They're probably too young to appreciate the beautiful things that are here.'' Letting her gaze circle the room, she added, ''Mr. Vandenburg has exquisite taste and apparently the money to go with it.''

''That he does,'' Kyle agreed wryly. ''Hugo will be delighted that you're helping the kids develop some appreciation for his hobby.''

Hobby? There was a sarcastic edge to Kyle's tone that surprised her. Perhaps he thought the field trip was a stupid idea.

As they started to leave the room, a miniature jeweled vase-shaped clock sitting on a small table began to chime the hour in clear bell-like tones. Ashley was instantly taken by the delicate beauty of the Oriental piece.

Ignoring Kyle's obvious impatience, she stopped to appreciate the exquisite antique. Sprays of emerald-green and ruby-red flowers adorned the front of the small clock, and amethysts ringed its rounded black base. She'd never seen anything so perfectly lovely. Entranced, she reached out and traced the beautiful curve of the gilded metal case with a fingertip.

"Don't even think about it." Rudy's ugly smile fastened on her. He stood a few feet away, just inside the door, watching. "Hugo's eagle eye will know if anything has been moved an inch. And if something turns up missing, well, let's just say he'd peel the skin from your bones and toss you out for the buzzards,'' he warned.

"Might be a good idea for you to heed your own warning, Rudy," Kyle answered shortly. "As far as Jill is concerned, I'm sure Hugo is going to be delighted with her knowledge and appreciation of the house and its furnishings." He gave Ashley a reassuring smile. "He's going to be surprised."

And so is Jill, Ashley thought. *I'm sorry, sis. I think I've really fouled up.* Without looking at either of the men, she walked out of the room and made her way down the hall to the swimming pool.

The children were already there and urged her to join them as they jumped into the pool.

"Not today," she said firmly, and dropped down in a lounge chair to watch them. Parading around in a bathing suit and showing off the scratched leg wasn't a good idea when she wanted everyone to forget about it as soon as possible.

She was still smarting from Rudy's pointed warning, and she wondered if Kyle had just happened to join her and the children or was he there to make sure she didn't steal something?

She winced as the thought struck her that he might actually have believed Hendrick's accusation that she was after the silver that other night. That would account for his sudden interest in joining the "field trip." Knowing that he didn't trust her hurt more than she was willing to admit. She hadn't realized how much his good opinion meant to her.

As soon as she could, she'd call Jill with the news that Hugo and some guests were due to arrive tomorrow evening in time for dinner. The time frame was going to be a tight one. Ashley's stomach felt queasy just thinking about it, but she was confident in Jill's ability to take things in her stride. More than once her twin had bluffed her way out of a tense situation when they were growing up, and Ashley doubted that she'd lost that ability as an adult.

Ashley listened to the children's squeals as they splashed each other and wrestled in the water for the ball, and she hoped the visit with their grandfather would go well. They obviously were afraid of him, and the children didn't seem to be the only ones. She sensed rising tension in almost everyone in the house. Even Kyle and Rudy seemed to be on edge.

Taking out a pencil and pad from her purse, she began to make a list of things that she must not forget to tell Jill. She prayed that her sister would have time to memorize all of them before she was plunged into the whirlpool of Hugo's visit.

After forty-five minutes, Ashley ordered, "Time to get out." Ignoring groans and protests, she herded Benny and Pamela up the back stairs and into their rooms. They'd have the rest of the afternoon to rest before Lily came after them for dinner.

Tomorrow at this time, Ashley knew she would have already left. She prayed that the household would be so busy getting ready for the expected guests that no one would pay any attention to her. Kyle and Hugo were her main worries.

As soon as Lily had left and Davie was happily cooing and sucking on his fists, Ashley took out the cell phone and, sitting on the bed, dialed Jill's number. When the answering machine came on, Ashley gave the usual message, hung up and dialed again.

Usually Jill picked up the phone before the third ring, and when she didn't answer after the sixth ring, Ashley decided Jill wasn't there. She knew she was calling earlier in the day than usual and was about to hang up before the answering machine came on again, when she heard a click and a breathless voice answered, "Yes…hello?"

Not Jill's voice. Ashley hesitated, afraid to identify herself.

"Hello…is anybody there?"

The impatient voice was suddenly familiar. "Hannah?"

"Yes, is this Ashley?"

"Yes."

"Oh, thank heavens you called."

The relief in the voice of Jill's neighbor was so obvious that Ashley's hand tightened on the phone. "What's wrong?"

"It's Jill. She got caught in the rain last evening. I told her it was no weather for her to be out shopping, but she insisted. Came home drenched to the bone. That bug she's been fighting got hold of her in the night, and she's back in bed, coughing her head off."

Ashley closed her eyes, praying that this wasn't

happening. Hannah had to be mistaken. Jill had to be here by tomorrow evening.

"She's sleeping right now. But she told me if you called to tell you that it will be a few more days before she's out and about." Hannah rattled on for another couple of minutes about Jill's situation and Budge before she sighed and said, "Him running off with all that money, and leaving her with nothing but bills. It makes you wonder what the world is coming to."

Ashley moistened her dry lips. "Hannah, thanks for looking after Jill. I really appreciate it."

"I called her doctor and got a new prescription for her. He told me to keep her in bed, give her aspirin and plenty of liquids. How are you and the baby getting along?"

"Fine, just fine." *F.I.N.E.—Feelings Inside Not Expressed.*

"Good. Jill says you're visiting relatives, and I think it's a good idea to keep the baby away until she gets over this."

"Yes, I think so, too. Give Jill my love and…and tell her not to worry."

"I will. You take care. Bye."

Ashley sat on the edge of the bed and stared unseeing at the floor. One thought revolved over and over again like a trapped animal running around in a wheel. Jill wasn't coming. Not tomorrow. Not for who-knew-how-long? She couldn't believe they weren't going to make the switch. There was only one thing that hadn't changed. Hugo Vandenburg would be here tomorrow.

From everything she'd learned about Hugo Vandenburg, no one in her right mind would try to make a fool out of him. She didn't know if Jill had spent any private time with the owner of her husband's basketball team, or if she'd just been one of the crowd. How could she attempt to carry on a sensible conversation without any inkling of what had passed between them? He'd publicly denounced Budge for his illegal betting, and offered a reward for information leading to his arrest. She knew that Hugo had made a special effort to help Jill by offering her this nanny job, so he must have some personal interest in her welfare.

She began to pace the floor. She couldn't do it. Pretending that she was Jill in front of a bunch of strangers was bad enough, but to be in close contact with someone who actually knew Jill was impossible. She would have to leave tomorrow as planned—only Jill wouldn't be taking her place. The charade was over.

"I just don't think I can pull it off," she said to Davie, gurgling and kicking in his crib. "What if Hugo knows right off the bat that I'm not your mother?"

Then we'll have to leave anyway.

The answer was so clear that she blinked to satisfy herself that it had come from her own mind. Then she laughed and tickled Davie's stomach.

"All right, I'll try," she whispered, as much to herself as to the baby.

Chapter Ten

"Don't you feel well?" Kyle asked Ashley at dinner. He'd made several attempts at conversation without much more than a perfunctory response on her part. She seemed to be miles away and was only playing with her food. Her lovely eyes were shadowed and her supple lips tensed, as if guarding some plaguing worry. The contrast with her high sparkling spirits that afternoon on the children's "field trip" made him wonder if she were ill.

"I'm fine."

"You don't seem fine."

"I guess I'm a little worried about Mr. Vandenburg's visit."

"Why? Just be yourself."

Ashley choked back a laugh. What would Kyle do if he knew the repercussions of that advice?

"Is something funny?" he asked, seeing a faint smile at the corners of her lips.

She shook her head, hating herself for deceiving him. He deserved better than her trickery. If only she could be honest with him, tell him why she had to protect Jill's job at all cost. Was there a chance that he would forgive her and help her over the next few days of Hugo's visit? There was no denying that she felt drawn to him on levels that she'd never felt before. A quivering excitement shot through her at his casual touch, and more than once she'd glimpsed something in his eyes that matched her own heightened awareness. Surely he would understand and agree to be her accomplice.

She cleared her throat, trying to find the right words to confess the charade she'd been playing. If Rudy hadn't come into the dining room at that moment, she might have gambled and admitted everything, but the whole timbre of the room changed with the unpleasant man's presence, and the chance for honesty slipped away.

"Sorry I'm late," Rudy said, but his careless manner belied the apology. "I had a few drinks at the Harbor Lounge and time got away from me." His breath had a sour odor and his face was flushed with liquor. Even so, he went straight to the bar to fix another drink. "I don't suppose you two missed me, though." His smile was a lewd suggestion as to what he thought they'd been up to while he was away.

"You better get your drinking done before Hugo gets here," Kyle answered sharply. Keeping Rudy under control when he was sober was hard enough; half-drunk, the man was pure meanness.

Ashley pushed away from the table. "I'll leave you

two men to enjoy your dinner. I'm really not hungry.''

"What's the matter, baby?" Rudy drawled. "You nervous about the boss coming? Are you afraid he'll want to taste a little of the sweetness you're spreading around?" Rudy winked at her. "The boss likes a bit of honey now and again."

"Shut up, Rudy," Kyle snapped. "Or I'll shove that dirty tongue of yours right down your throat."

Rudy just laughed. "Kinda touchy, aren't you? I wonder how the boss is going to react to this little game you two have got going."

Ashley didn't wait to hear any more. If the two men came to blows, she didn't want to see it. Thank heavens, she hadn't spilled anything to Kyle. Whatever had made her think he would support her in the deception she was playing on all of them? she wondered as she rushed from the room and headed upstairs.

When she came into the nursery, Lily looked up in surprise. She had Davie on her lap, rocking him. "You can't be through with dinner this fast," she said.

"I wasn't hungry."

"You don't look good. Are you nervous about Mr. Vandenburg coming tomorrow?" the young woman asked with surprising perception.

"Should I be nervous?" Ashley wasn't above pumping the maid for as much insight as she could get. Jill had spoken so highly of Hugo that Ashley'd never questioned for a moment that his gesture to her was anything but benevolent concern. Now she wondered. Was Hugo low enough to expect an expression of her gratitude? She wanted to believe that it was just Rudy's foul mind working overtime. Still it wouldn't hurt to know everything about her boss that she could. Maybe Hugo's offer of a job wasn't as benign as Jill thought.

"Well, sometimes Mr. Vandenburg fires people when they don't please him or Mrs. Borsch. But Mr. Stone likes you, and he'll put in a good word for you." Lily hesitated as if she'd like to say more but didn't dare.

Ashley had no trouble reading her unspoken words. Mrs. Borsch was ready to get Jill Gordon fired. This didn't surprise Ashley. The housekeeper had made her dislike evident from the first day, and the fiasco with Hendrick had added fuel to the woman's antipathy. No telling what rumors Mrs. Borsch had started about Ashley and Kyle over the lighthouse incident, and Rudy was certain to have helped the gossip along. No wonder the nanny's job was in jeopardy.

What will Jill think if I get fired from her job? Trying to find another one with a dismissal and no references would only add to her twin's tough times. As much as Ashley hated thinking about continuing the deception, for Jill's and the baby's sakes, she couldn't get sacked. She'd have to do everything she could to offset the bad reports she was sure to get from Mrs. Borsch, Hendrick and Rudy.

KYLE WAS FURIOUS with Rudy for taunting Jill with Hugo's appetite for sexy women, and he was angry with himself for the rage that consumed him just thinking about his boss putting his lecherous hands on her. How could he stand by and watch Hugo manipulate her for his own selfish satisfaction? He knew how much Jill needed this job; what he didn't know was how much she would do to keep it. If he interfered in Hugo's amorous advances in any way, he could easily jeopardize the whole situation.

Rudy eyed Kyle's thunderous face with malicious satisfaction. "Let me give you some advice, Romeo Boy. Don't go all heroic on us. You get in the boss's way and you'll know what a bug feels like crushed under foot."

"And don't you be spreading your filth in his ears," warned Kyle.

"There are plenty around here that'll do that for me," Rudy answered smugly.

Kyle knew that Mrs. Borsch was ready to fill Hugo's ear with suspicions that something was going on between him and the nanny. Thank goodness Jill had never been to the cottage, or it would be all over the house that he was sleeping with her. The few times they'd been away from the house, except for the lighthouse incident, the children had been with them.

He'd tell Hugo that he'd kept a close eye on her the way he'd ordered, and that was that. He just hoped he could hide the deep attraction that he felt for her and keep her safe when the showdown came. If things went badly with Hugo, he didn't dare think about the consequences.

THE NEXT MORNING the children were both irritable and listless. They must have had the same kind of restless night as she'd had, Ashley decided. She'd been caught up in a nightmare that seemed to have no end. Kyle's angry voice followed her as she fled through the forest. He blocked her way at every turn. Was the dream trying to tell her not to trust Kyle Stone?

The impending arrival of Hugo permeated the whole house, making the library seem confining and dreary. The children's enthusiasm for writing stories and making books had disappeared, and Ashley had a hard time concentrating on anything herself.

"Let's forget about doing any writing today," she said as she handed out some paper and colored pencils.

"What are these for?" Benny demanded suspiciously.

"We're going to take another field trip,"

Pamela's eyes brightened, but her brother grumbled. "Not the house again."

"I want to see what kind of artists you are. We're going to draw instead of write." She picked up some books on southern flowers and plants, and led the way to the solarium.

Joseph scowled at them when they came in. He'd been rearranging some of the potted plants and furniture, and Ashley could see that he'd added some chairs and round tables near a small waterfall that was banked by rocks and flowering shrubs. "I got everything just the way the boss likes it. Don't you be messing up the place."

"We won't," Ashley promised. "We won't touch anything." She smiled at the children to punctuate her assurance. "Now choose a flower or tree and make a sketch of it," Ashley instructed them. "In pencil first and then put in some color. When you've finished, find the flower or plant in one of these books. Identify it and write down a little bit about it."

"Are you going to draw, too?" Benny asked suspiciously.

Ashley nodded.

"Okay." To her surprise, Benny immediately plopped down in front of a ceramic swan filled with yellow lilies, and, scrunching up his mouth in concentration, he began to draw. Pamela took her time looking around and finally chose the waterfall and the banked flowers around it.

After a moment of scowling scrutiny, Joseph seemed satisfied that the kids weren't going to tear up the place. When he'd finished his chores, he gave Ashley a brief nod and left. Relieved that the art lessons seemed to be going well, she sat down in a lounge chair that was far enough away to give Pamela and Benny some privacy but close enough for them to feel her company. She didn't want them to think she was looking over their shoulders at every stroke of their pencils.

Dappled sunlight coming through the glass roof

and the melodious trickling of the waterfall began to have a soothing effect on Ashley's jangled nerves. Her chair was placed near a collection of potted orchids that Joseph had gathered together, and she decided to sketch a fuschia-tipped pink orchid, even though she would have preferred to lean her head against the back of the chair and close her eyes. Every nerve in her body was frayed in nervous anticipation of Hugo's arrival.

She wasn't aware that anyone had come into the room behind her, and she jumped when she felt warm breath on her neck. Kyle leaned over her shoulder. "Very nice."

She immediately stiffened.

"Sorry if I startled you," he apologized.

She continued to shade the green leaves of her drawing without answering. He was a reminder of the narrow precipice that she was walking. Just being with him put her emotions in a tangle. How could she act naturally when her composure was splintered with worry and doubt?

"I checked the library, and when you weren't there, I thought I'd track you down and see what exciting things you and the children were up to this morning." The truth was that Kyle had been worried about her reaction to what Rudy had said about Hugo putting the make on her. He could tell from the faint shadows under her eyes that she hadn't slept well.

Impulsively, he walked over to the potted orchids, broke off the pink blossom she was drawing and handed it to her. "You deserve the real thing."

"You shouldn't have. Joseph will throw a fit," she said in a hushed voice.

"Let him."

"You're a lot braver than I am."

"I'll pick you a whole bouquet if you'd like," he said recklessly.

"Oh, no, please. One orchid is enough to get me in all kinds of trouble."

"I'll be your protector," he announced.

She gazed at the orchid for a long minute and then raised wide, searching eyes to his face. "I may need one."

The pleading look in her eyes took him by surprise. She was deeply disturbed about something.

"It's just a flower," he said, trying to make light of her obvious discomfort. He guessed that Hugo's impending visit was responsible for her apprehension, but there was little he could do to change that. If she only knew that the boss's visit entailed all kinds of risks for all of them...but in the end, Kyle had no choice but to demonstrate complete loyalty to his boss.

"Don't pay any attention to Rudy's foul mouth," Kyle said abruptly. "It's very unlikely that Hugo will come on to you in any inappropriate way." He silently prayed that that was true.

"I can handle myself," Ashley assured him, but could she handle Hugo the way Jill would? Her sister knew how to keep a man's attention and enjoy a light flirtation without committing herself to anything serious. Ashley had always watched in amazement the way Jill collected and discarded admirers without ever letting herself get really involved. Budge was the first one to capture her love and devotion, and Ashley would never forgive him for treating Jill so shabbily.

"Hugo likes beautiful women, and he likes to show them off," he warned her. "He may want you to play the guitar and sing for his guests."

"I...I'm too rusty," she stammered as her heart plunged like a roller coaster in a deep dive. What if Hugo insisted? Any refusal would embarrass him, and she knew he wouldn't take that lightly. It might even be the cue he needed to recognize the fraud that she was.

At that moment the children saw Kyle and eagerly showed him their artistic efforts.

"Great job." Taking time to look carefully at each one, he told them how good their drawings were and teased them about selling their work when they got to be famous artists.

"Grandfather wouldn't like it," Pamela said solemnly.

"Are you sure?" Kyle gave her a warm smile.

The little girl nodded. "My mother says Grandfather doesn't want anyone in the family to have money but him. She says we have to do what he says."

A muscle in Kyle's cheek tightened. "Well, maybe when you're a big girl, things will be different."

"Mama's a big girl and she has to do what he says—" Pamela's voice quivered and her eyes suddenly glistened with tears. "Like sending us here for the summer."

"It's all right, honey." He exchanged a quick look with Ashley as he gently stroked Pamela's dark head. "You're having a good summer, aren't you? You've got a pretty nanny who thinks up all kinds of great things for you to do. I bet you're having more fun here than at home."

"I am," Benny said with enthusiasm. "This is a lot better than summer school, like last year."

The insight the children were giving about their grandfather certainly wasn't a flattering one, Ashley thought, and it was obvious that their parents were under his thumb.

"It's almost time for lunch," she said, looking at her watch.

Kyle laughed. "I almost forgot. That's what I came to ask you. How about lunch on the beach? The kitchen's in turmoil, and I managed to get Gerta to fix us a basket. We'd be better off getting out of the house for a while. What do you think?" he asked Ashley.

"Would you mind just taking Benny and Pamela?" she asked. "I don't feel up to the sun and water today. What time do you expect Mr. Vandenburg?"

"We're not sure. Sometime before dinner. Mrs. Borsch is preparing the main dining room for twelve."

Ashley's heart plummeted. How many of those people had Jill met?

Seeing her tense expression, he touched her arm. "Maybe you should rest. When Hugo brings guests, he expects us all to play host."

"Really?" she asked with a catch in her throat. "Even me?"

He nodded. "Hugo will want you to circulate so you'll want to be at your gracious best."

She wanted to laugh at that. *My gracious best or Jill's?*

"I'll try to make the best impression I can."

"Go get some rest, and I'll manage the kids for a couple of hours." Impulsively, he bent and kissed her lightly on the forehead. If anyone needed to be held and cosseted, she did, and the brotherly kiss might have turned into much more if he hadn't held himself back. He quickly turned to the kids. "Come on, let's get our suits and head for the beach."

A few minutes later, when Ashley came into the nursery holding the orchid, Lily's eyes widened in horror. "Oh, my goodness. Mr. Vandenburg never allows anyone to pick his prize orchids."

"I didn't pick it. Kyle did." She smiled, remembering how gallantly he had offered it to her.

"Oh, well, I guess it's all right then," Lily said, letting out her breath. "I guess Mr. Stone really likes you. Do you like him?"

"He seems nice enough," she answered casually, hiding the truth that she was very attracted to him. Since that first day in the pool, she'd been lying to herself about her growing feelings for him. Totally conscious of her deceit, she'd tried to cover her guilt by denying that she even liked him. Now she knew that her feelings had somehow slipped beyond just the liking stage. The way he made her feel when he was close to her created a bewildering longing and hunger to be in his arms. How ironic it would be if she had waited until now to fall in love with someone who would never know who she really was.

"Well, I think Mr. Stone is a very nice person," Lily said with a defiant lift of her red head. "And I don't believe for a minute the things they say about him. Mrs. Borsch and Hendrick are afraid of him, you know, but I'm not. I don't think it's true, do you?"

"What?" Ashley's mouth was suddenly dry.

"That he killed someone."

Chapter Eleven

"I don't believe it. It has to be a lie." Ashley had seen anger flash in Kyle's dark eyes when Rudy was taunting him, but she'd never ever believe he was capable of killing anyone.

"That's what I was thinking."

"If he'd killed someone, he'd be in prison," Ashley argued, trying to ignore a sick quivering in the pit of her stomach.

"Mrs. Borsch said there was some kind of mistrial. That's when Mr. Stone came to work for Mr. Vandenburg in New York." Lily lowered her voice. "Then all of a sudden the boss sends him here for the summer. Kinda strange, isn't it? You'd think Mr. Stone would have more important things to do than just overseeing this place, wouldn't you?"

"The thought has crossed my mind," Ashley admitted. Suddenly she felt like someone standing on a ship with the deck boards breaking apart under her. Kyle—a killer? If she couldn't trust him to be what he seemed, whom could she trust?

"I shouldn't be telling you all of this," Lily said, suddenly anxious. "I could get the sack for talking out of line. If you say anything—"

"I won't. Don't worry, Lily. I'm glad to have someone in the house who's my friend. Let's just forget we had this conversation, okay?"

"Okay." As she started toward the door, Lily said, "I bet if you asked Mr. Stone, he'd explain everything."

Ashley didn't answer. How could she tell the young woman that sometimes the truth was the last thing you wanted anyone to know?

She waited until mid-afternoon before she called Jill, and was relieved when her sister's husky voice answered their pre-arranged signal.

"Thank goodness," Ashley said, relieved. "Jill, how are you?"

"Can't you tell?" she croaked. "I can't believe this is happening. I was almost over the other bug, and now this. What a crock."

"Well, the situation's gotten worse since we last talked. Hugo is due to arrive this afternoon with a bunch of guests." She couldn't keep the sarcasm out of her voice. "Lovely, isn't it? Now all I have to do is fool him and who knows how many others. He may even want me to play the guitar and sing for him, how about that?"

"Oh, my gosh." Jill gulped.

"How well do you know Hugo? What conversations have you had with him? I feel as if I have my hands tied behind my back. The wrong word out of my mouth and this whole charade could fall apart. If that happens, both Davie and I will be out on our ear in short order.''

"Please don't let that happen, Ashley." Jill's froggy voice broke. "You can handle it. I know you can."

"How can I handle anything if I don't know what to say or do? Jill, how well do you know Vandenburg?"

"Not well at all," she assured Ashley. "When he entertained the team, Budge and I went to some parties and he was there. I was nice to him, that's all."

"Nice?" What was Jill's definition of "nice"?

"You know, nice. Smiled. Chatted a little bit about nothing. Usually there'd be a bunch of people around, and once Hugo took a few of the players and their wives for a short cruise on his yacht. We had a good time."

Ashley groaned. "Where did you go?"

"I don't know. Just around. It doesn't matter, does it? For heaven's sake, sis, he's not going to give you the third degree. Just be friendly, that's all."

"How friendly, Jill? Did he ever come on to you in a sexual way?"

"With Budge around?" She croaked a laugh. "Not hardly. Sure, he flirted with me a little, but he always brought along his own paramours. Budge would have knocked him into orbit if he'd fooled around with me."

But Budge won't be around. He deserted you, remember?

"What about the rest of the people who might be coming with Hugo? Could there be someone who knows you pretty well?"

"I don't think so. Budge introduced me to a lot of people but I don't even remember their names. I doubt if they remember mine."

Ashley sighed. "Let's hope you're right."

"Just relax, sis. And have a good time. That's what I would do. Won't this Stone fellow be around?"

"Have you ever heard any rumors about him, Jill? Try to remember," she said with a queasy feeling in her stomach.

"I told you, I never met him. He must have worked with Hugo in New York."

"And you've never heard any...rumors about him?"

"I never heard his name until you told me he was on the island. What's the matter with you, anyway? You're not setting me up for any kind of intimate relationship with this guy, are you?"

"No, of course not."

After talking to Jill, Ashley felt worse than before about the challenges facing her in a few hours. She'd gotten very little help in how to relate to Hugo, and had learned absolutely nothing about Kyle. She shouldn't have been surprised. Growing up, her sister had always been concerned with her own little world, and plenty of things had slipped by her without catching Jill's interest.

Ashley was sure that the handsome Kyle would have captured her attention if she'd ever met him. Jill would be lucky to have him around. It would be her twin who would be spending the summer with Kyle. Thinking about the things they would be doing together, Ashley wondered how long Jill's dedication to her missing husband would last when Kyle picked orchids for her and gave her warm hugs.

Ashley took herself in hand. *Don't think about it.* This was no time to be jealous of her sister. She had a decisive challenge facing her, one that could easily explode in her face with one wrong word or action.

When Pamela poked her head into the nursery later in the afternoon, the little girl's expression was anxious.

"Grandfather's here. Are you coming down to meet him?" she asked anxiously, obviously hoping Ashley would go downstairs with her and Benny.

"No, I'll meet him at dinner." Ashley gave her an encouraging smile. "I'm sure he'll be happy to see you and Benny."

"He scares me."

"I know." *He scares me, too.* Impulsively Ashley hugged the little girl. "I'll bet if you give him one of your sweet smiles, he'll smile right back."

Pamela looked skeptical and left the room with dragging steps. Ashley wondered if there was anyone in the household who'd be happy about being under the same roof as Hugo Vandenburg.

ASHLEY LOOKED OVER Jill's limited wardrobe and changed her mind three times about what she should wear. Finally, she decided that the red dress she'd worn to dinner the first night was the one she'd feel the most comfortable wearing. What did it matter if Kyle and the staff had already seen it? Her concern was Hugo and his guests. Even though Ashley knew that Jill probably would have chosen something more flashy, like the beaded fuschia sweater and matching suede skirt, Ashley decided on the red sheath, and wearing gold jewelry instead of silver gave it a richer look.

Brushing her amber hair into a smooth French swirl that curled on the top of her head, she softened the look with a few wispy tendrils curling around her face. As she started to put on her makeup, she realized that, unwittingly, the last few days, she'd fallen more into her normal habit of less mascara and eye shadow, and only a light touch of lipstick. Tonight she would have to make sure her makeup matched her sister's as closely as possible. Hugo was bound to notice any change in the way Jill looked.

Deliberately, Ashley made use of everything in her twin's cosmetic bag except the artificial eyelashes. She decided that her own lashes were long and thick enough to accent her eyes. By the time she'd finished, and surveyed herself in the mirror, she was sure that all signs of the colorless Ashley Camdon had been erased.

"Wow," said Lily when she came in to watch the baby so Ashley could go down to dinner. "I love your hair that way. You're going to knock 'em out. Even Mr. Vandenburg's *new* friend isn't half as pretty as you are."

"New friend?"

Lily wrinkled up her nose. "One of those skinny, beanpole women. You're a lot prettier, and you should have heard what the children were saying about you. I think Mr. Vandenburg was really surprised."

Was that good or bad? Ashley asked silently. "How did things go with the children? I know Pamela was nervous about seeing her grandfather."

Lily shrugged. "Well, he didn't act like my granddad. No hugs or kisses or anything like that. If you ask me, I don't think he likes being old enough to have grandkids. He just asked them polite questions as if they belonged to someone else's family. I kinda felt sorry for the kids. They were plenty glad to get out of the room when he let them go."

Not a very reassuring report.

"Well, I guess I'd better go down and meet the boss," she said as lightly as she could. "I'd better not be late for dinner."

"They're having drinks in the living room," Lily told her.

Let the show begin.

Ashley's hands were moist and her mouth dry as she went downstairs. She walked slowly, taking several deep breaths to settle her nerves, and was almost to the open doorway of the spacious living room when she stopped short.

I don't know what Hugo looks like!

How could she walk into a roomful of people and pretend to know her boss when she'd never seen him?

If there were photos of Hugo Vandenburg around the house, they must be in his den or some room that she hadn't found. As luck would have it, she'd never even seen a newspaper photo of him.

Lily said he didn't like being taken for a grandfather. Did that mean he might be the most youthful-looking man in the group? What if she smiled at the wrong person? What if he took offense because she didn't rush up to him with bubbly greetings. What if—

"Jill, wait."

She turned around and stiffened when she saw Kyle hurrying toward her from the far end of the hall. Even though she had tried to convince herself that Lily had just been passing on some vicious gossip, she couldn't help but view him with sudden apprehension. How could she trust him under the circumstances?

"I guess we're a little late," Kyle gave her an easy smile. He was wearing a white dinner jacket, dark slacks, white shirt and bow tie. The shine in his dark hair was evidence of a recent shampooing and quick brushing. "I got hung up on the telephone and didn't allow myself enough time. We'd better hurry and join the others. Hugo doesn't like stragglers."

How does he feel about impostors? The unspoken question was like the jab of a sharp prong in her chest.

Kyle saw the dark veiling of her eyes and said, "Hey, relax. You look like someone about to go before a judge for sentencing."

"Maybe I am," she answered dryly.

"Hey, Hugo really likes you or he wouldn't have

offered you the nanny job," he lied smoothly. He fervently hoped that her behavior would assure Hugo that there wasn't any danger of her leaving before the trap was sprung. Kyle knew that if she made waves for herself she'd be inviting the kind of crude pressuring that Rudy was itching to put on her. "Just enjoy yourself."

"I'll try," she said and managed a weak smile, silently relieved that she didn't have to go into the living room alone. Now she could identify Hugo without betraying herself.

Kyle put a light, reassuring touch on her arm and guided her into the spacious living room where Hugo's guests were clustered in a conversational grouping at one end of the room.

Ashley's heart nearly stopped when she saw three gentlemen in evening dress rise from their chairs at her approach.

Which one was Hugo? Any one of them was about the right age to be the children's grandfather.

She shot a quick glance at Kyle, and saw him nodding at the robust, thick-shouldered man in the center. Even though he wasn't as tall as the other two men beside him, he somehow over-shadowed them.

Slightly wavy dark hair was touched with silver gray and his face was squarish with strong, boldly handsome features. His lips curved into a smile that didn't reach the arctic-cold blue of his eyes. As his gaze traveled over Ashley, there was something sensual about the man, like a handsome despot who could condemn with a soft intimate smile as easily as

he could praise. There was no doubt in Ashley's mind
that this was Hugo Vandenburg.

"Sorry we're a bit late," Kyle said with obvious
deference to his boss.

Still smiling, Hugo ignored him and held out a di-
amond-studded hand to Ashley. "Jill, my darling.
How wonderful to see you."

Even his voice had a soft, sensuous purr about it,
she thought, returning his smile. As she put her hand
in his, he pulled her slightly towards him, and instinctively she placed the expected light kiss on his cheek.

A heavy scent of expensive men's cologne mingled
with spicy hair tonic quivered her nostrils. He wore
a tailored black dinner jacket, white pleated shirt with
diamond cuff links and trousers accented with black
satin stripes down each side. The breadth of his chest
was matched by the broad expanse of his hips and
thighs, and the evening attire could not hide the genes
passed on to him by his Germanic forefathers.

"You're looking as handsome as ever, Hugo,"
Ashley said, trying to mimic Jill's light flirtatious
manner. "It's great to see you again. I can't tell you
how wonderful it is to be here." Some detached part
of her mind was monitoring her remarks and measuring them. She feared that they sounded as hollow and
false to him as they did to her.

"It's our pleasure, my dear. My grandchildren have
been praising you to the highest."

"Pamela and Benny are very sweet. They both
have very sharp minds." She caught herself as she
was about to extol their intellectual abilities. This

kind of evaluation was not in line with her sister's
capabilities or interest. "We've been having a good
time doing all kinds of fun things," she said with a
light laugh.

Under dark, rigid eyebrows his grayish-blue eyes
remained so coldly appraising that she could almost
see herself reflected in them. Her breath caught. What
was the matter? Had he seen through her already?

One of the men at Hugo's side spoke up. "We've
all been looking forward to meeting the fantastic Jill
Gordon. How about introductions, Hugo?"

Ashley's inner turmoil was so great that none of
the names made the slightest dent in her mind as
Hugo did his duty as host and introduced her to the
gathering of about eight people. As they moved
among his guests, she was grateful that none of them
made any reference to having met Jill before.

She intercepted a couple of looks between some of
the women and guessed that they knew the circumstances of her being there. They looked her over as
if to say, *You're damn lucky that Hugo took you in
after what your husband did.* None of them seemed
to expect Ashley to join in the conversation, so she
just smiled and said little.

Kyle handed her a pink drink with a knowing
smile. "Just the way you like it."

Great, thought Ashley. Just what she needed, a
strong drink to dull her wits when every word out of
her mouth could prove disastrous. She was glad that
the other guests were engaging Hugo in conversation.

"You're doing fine," he said softly, out of the corner of his mouth, and then turned to speak to one of the women guests.

She was grateful for his encouragement, even though she knew he wouldn't be as supportive if he knew the truth about her.

As Kyle melted into the background, Ashley did her best to look perfectly at ease as she sipped her drink and kept a practiced smile on her face.

A woman introduced as Betts Tompson was the only guest who showed any kind of personal interest in her. It was obvious that she was weighing her up as competition for Hugo's attention.

She was clearly the skinny beanpole that Lily had mentioned. A bleached blonde, she wore a clinging gold-sequined dress with a slit in the long draped skirt that revealed a long, shapely leg. Her lips were carefully drawn in ruby gloss lipstick and her eyelashes dripped with ebony mascara. There wasn't an ounce of fat on her lean body, and she looked as if she hadn't had a decent meal in a year. Something in her eyes made Ashley think of a hungry predator.

"So you're a special friend of Hugo's," she said, raising a thin, carefully plucked black eyebrow in a questioning manner.

"Budge played on his team for a couple of years," Ashley answered evenly, sipping her drink. "Do you follow basketball?" she asked, quickly tossing the conversation back in the woman's lap.

Betts made a face. "I find the whole business of running up and down a court perfectly boring," she responded, flicking her cigarette ashes into a porcelain dish that must have cost Hugo a goodly sum. Ashley winced to see ugly ashes covering a beautiful inlaid mosaic pattern. "I suppose there are some women who take it seriously."

"I guess it's the lifestyle that makes it glamorous and exciting for all of us," Ashley said, hoping that the remark fitted in with something her sister might say.

Betts leveled piercing brown eyes at Ashley. "Maybe it's competition that puts life into any game, and I've always prided myself on being a winner."

Ashley wanted to laugh. The challenge was clear enough.

Did the woman really believe that Jill would be the least bit interested in competing for the amorous attentions of Hugo Vandenburg?

How ridiculous!

Did people think that his benevolence to a deserted wife had an ulterior motive to it? His offer of the nanny's job was a kind gesture, she tried to reassure herself, but when Hugo turned away from the couple with whom he'd been conversing and came over to her, she mentally stiffened.

"I believe dinner is ready. Shall we go in, Jill?" he asked in a polite but possessive tone.

He offered his arm, and Ashley didn't dare refuse. There was absolutely nothing she could do but set down her drink and let him escort her out of the room. She felt Betts's hostile glare on her and was aware of Kyle watching as if measuring her reaction to his boss's pointed attention.

As the rest of the company followed them out of the room, she was suddenly aware that Rudy had been absent from the gathering. Thank heavens for small favors, she breathed prayerfully. Putting up with Rudy's lewd looks and crude remarks was more than she could handle at the moment.

Hugo was only a few inches taller than she, but he walked like a potentate at the head of a procession. They crossed the center hall to the magnificent dining room with the fluted high ceiling, embossed gold wallpaper and two chandeliers fashioned with dangling showers of crystals. The long table was beautifully set with antique china and silver.

"What a gorgeous room," Ashley breathed. It was even more magnificent than the first time she'd seen it as the maids were getting it ready.

A flicker of pleasure crossed Hugo's face, and he looked at her with some surprise. "I didn't know you had an appreciation for vintage furnishings. I would have thought that the modern style suited you much better."

Ashley tried a light laugh that she hoped would cover her immediate consternation while she searched for something flippant to say. In that instant she realized that sooner or later, he would hear about the field trip she'd taken with Pamela and Benny through the house.

"The children and I have been gaining some appreciation for all the wonderful things you have in the house. I confess I've never been exposed to such surroundings. It's really an education to live in a place like this.'' That much was true. Living with the real thing was different from looking at pictures or visiting a museum.

''I take pride in my collections,'' he told her. ''And I don't keep them under lock and key because I intend to enjoy them. No one under my roof has ever betrayed that trust.'' She read a warning in his eyes that was obviously meant for no one but herself.

He'd heard about the fiasco with the pantry silver.

She felt heat rising into her face, and choked back a sharp rebuttal to his pointed warning as they took their places. Hugo sat at the head of the long table, and he had placed her in the first chair on his right side.

Other guests took their places; the tall man whose name she'd already forgotten took the chair beside her. Another male guest took the chair on the other side of the table at Hugo's left, across from her.

Ashley fixed a polite smile on her face and wished to heaven she were anywhere but at this dinner party. Her sister was going to owe her a lifetime of favors for all of this. How in the world could she get through this evening without betraying her true feelings—and her true identity?

Ashley experienced a moment of regret when Kyle escorted Betts to the foot of the table and took the first chair on the side, on her right. At a signal from Hugo, waiting servants moved to the table with their offerings of wine and the first course of an elaborate dinner. Apparently the extra help were professionals, because their serving was very smooth and unobtrusive.

Ashley didn't see Gerta at all, and suspected that she was helping Hendrick in the kitchen. Once she thought she caught a glimpse of Mrs. Borsch through a swinging door, but she wasn't sure.

Hugo offered little in the way of conversation during the course of the dinner. He concentrated on eating as if he were a man who loved good food and wanted to enjoy it without interruption. Once in a while he'd glance down the length of the table where his dinner guests were creating a low murmur of conversation as they enjoyed the five-course meal. Hendrick had outdone himself, preparing a crab-and-artichoke appetizer, chilled strawberry soup, scallopini of pork tenderloin, wild rice and sautéed carrots.

The man on Ashley's right made some polite remarks about the wine and food, but didn't try to engage her in any conversation. The woman next to him chatted with him about some mutual acquaintances that they had in New York.

Ashley's gaze kept drifting down the table to where Kyle was leaning forward, laughing and talking with Betts as if they were at a private dinner party with just the two of them. Once he caught her eyes on him before she could jerk them away, and she flushed when he flashed her a quick smile. Most of the time she gave her attention to the meal that landed heavily in her nervous stomach.

Kyle could tell that she was finding the dinner an

ordeal. Betts glared at him when she intercepted one of the reassuring glances he was trying to send to Ashley down the long table.

"So she has you dancing to her tune, too. The only two eligible men in the place can't keep their eyes off her," she said pettily. "I didn't agree to come here for this weekend so I could be ignored."

"Nobody's ignoring you, Betts. After all, you're sitting in the chair of honor, opposite the host," Kyle reasoned.

As he tried to placate the jealous Betts, reassuring her that Hugo was only being polite to the new nanny, he knew better. Hugo never did anything without an ulterior motive, and the bottom line was that Jill Gordon was important to his boss's plans. Hugo had deliberately placed her so that no one else would dare to monopolize her attention, but he seemed to be deliberately ignoring her.

What was more puzzling to Kyle was Jill's behavior. He'd heard Budge's wife really blossomed in any social gathering, fully enjoying herself and livening up the dullest affair. As far as he could tell, she was not living up to her reputation as a party girl at all. In fact, she was acting like a dud. Why wasn't she showering her charm on Hugo? Why wasn't she interacting with the men seated near her?

These questions pricked at him as he half-heartedly listened to Betts's empty chatter. Something was going on that he didn't understand. His gut feelings held a warning, and he'd learned the hard way to trust his intuition.

Dinner was almost over when Hugo leaned back in his chair and studied Ashley. ''Do you want to tell me what's wrong, Jill?''

A bite of cherries jubilee stuck in her throat, and she hastily took a swallow of water. Her thoughts reeled in every direction.

Here it comes. What do I do now?

She lightly touched a napkin to her lips and managed a smile. ''What do you mean? Nothing's the matter.''

''You don't seem yourself.''

She shrugged. ''I guess I'm a little stunned by all that has happened.''

''Aren't we all?'' he said coldly.

She struggled not to wither under his steady gaze. This was the moment that she'd been dreading. Was he sensing that there was something amiss? Maybe a slight deviation in facial structure that was almost imperceptible?

He studied her for a long moment as if she were a specimen under a microscope. Then his lips curved in a smile that lacked any warmth. ''I think it's time we had a nice private talk, don't you?''

Chapter Twelve

Hugo had arranged for after-dinner drinks to be served on the terrace, and as his guests made their way out of the dining room, he made no effort to single Ashley out.

"We'll talk tomorrow," he told her and then pointedly gave his attention to Betts who visibly brightened as he walked down the hall with her and settled her beside him at one of the patio tables. Betts flashed a superior smile at Ashley as if to gloat that Hugo must have found her company so wanting at dinner, he didn't want to waste any more time on her.

Even though Ashley felt an overwhelming flood of relief, she couldn't help but wish that he hadn't put off their little talk. Now she would have another sleepless night to worry about whether she could handle the private interview. She shivered just thinking about the kind of grilling that Hugo could put her through.

From all indications, he knew Jill a lot better than her twin had thought. She shivered just thinking about what Hugo's reaction would be if he found out that she was playing him for a fool by switching places with her twin.

"It's a warm night," Kyle said when he approached her on the terrace and saw her shiver. "Aren't you feeling well?"

"Not really," she said honestly. "I think I'll go to bed as soon as I can gracefully excuse myself."

"Oh, that's too bad. It's a lovely night," he said smoothly. "Why don't we sit down in the lounge chairs, and enjoy a nightcap?"

Kyle was under orders to keep her away from her room as long as possible. Despite Kyle's assurance that he had already searched Jill's bedroom and found the phone, Rudy was determined to satisfy his curiosity.

Kyle was puzzled that she had not used any of the house telephones after he had sabotaged her cell phone. She'd talked to someone the first night she was here, and he'd reasoned that if she'd been in touch with any since she would have used one of the bugged house telephones. So far, that hadn't happened. She hadn't made any calls, and he doubted that Rudy's search would reveal anything of importance. They knew that Lily usually dropped off to sleep in the nursery after she put the baby down, so Rudy would have a few stealthy minutes to give the bedroom a once-over.

"I don't feel like another drink," she said as they stood at the terrace railing. The last thing in the world she wanted was to get trapped into talking to any of the guests who were circulating with drinks in their hands. "I think I'll just enjoy a short walk in the garden."

"Good idea. After that huge meal I could use some exercise," he said, as if she'd invited his company.

"Oh, I don't want to take you away from the other guests," she said quickly. "Hugo might not like it."

Was she trying to slip away by herself? For some nefarious purpose, perhaps? He wasn't about to let her out of his sight. "I don't think you need to worry about Hugo." He gave a light chuckle. "You can tell that Betts has spread out her seductive web, and I'm sure we won't even be missed."

When Kyle put a firm guiding hand on her arm, Ashley knew that there was nothing she could do but accept his company. She wasn't about to create any kind of a scene. As they went down the steps into the garden, she couldn't help but be grateful for the strength radiating from his firm muscular body.

"I'm glad the weather cleared up."

"Yes, it's nice tonight," she said, following his lead into small talk. She could have moved away from the warmth of his possessive touch as they walked together, but she didn't. Her inner resources had dwindled to a low ebb. She was dangerously near the point of needing to confide in someone.

When Kyle looked at her and smiled, Ashley's emotions were pulled in several directions. She knew her feelings for Kyle Stone were not rational. She should be keeping her distance from him if Lily's rumor about him were true. How could she know what went on behind that engaging smile of his? Maybe it was true that he was hiding a despicable crime. How could she possibly even be thinking about telling him the truth? Common sense told her that trusting anyone in Hugo's employment was utter stupidity. Drawing a deep breath, she kept her gaze away from his, and tried to ignore the warring emotions that his nearness evoked.

Her deep sigh caused Kyle to search her profile. What kind of anxiety was deepening the shadows in her lovely face? Beautiful in the soft glow of moonlight, she had an ethereal quality about her. Her honey-colored hair was piled high on her head, and the style emphasized the lovely harmony of her face and perfect balance of her delicate features. He knew he was like a miser, hoarding these moments with her. At any minute, the carefully constructed scenario could be shattered, and he'd be left with an emptiness that would never again be filled. She had created a kind of joy within him that had made him a stranger to himself.

Small lights dotted stone paths that curved through the tropical garden, winding past marble statuary, lush flower beds and limpid pools reflecting moonlight from a clear sky. The southern moon brushed a golden patina on trees and bushes.

As they passed a camellia plant loaded with white blossoms, Kyle broke one off. "A beautiful flower for a beautiful lady."

She looked startled, as if he'd pulled her back from the edge of some dark abyss. For a moment he thought she was going to refuse to take the camellia. She stared at the flower in his hand as if she were struggling to reject his gesture.

"You don't like camellias?"

She moistened her lips. "I love them but—"

"But what?"

"I don't think you should be giving me flowers."

"Why not, Jill?"

Because I'm not Jill. Her lips moved, but no words came out. Her hand trembled slightly as she took the flower and raised it to her face. As she drew in the sweet fragrance, tears began to fill her eyes and she blinked rapidly to hold them back. She came close to telling him then. She wanted more than anything for this moment to be hers alone. Never had she felt so emotionally drawn to someone who would never know who she really was. She buried her nose in the fragrant petals, afraid to look at him.

Kyle saw the glistening of tears on her cheeks, and cursed himself for making a gesture that had only deepened her anxiety. He'd intended to please her, not make her cry. His voice was husky as he touched her cheek with a stroking fingertip. "I promise not to pick any more flowers if you promise not to cry."

She gave him a weak smile. "It's a deal."

Somewhere in the depths of the garden a night-bird's song floated from the high branches of a magnolia tree. Kyle slipped his arm through hers, and they walked to the edge of the garden where a panoramic view of the private beach lay below. Silver splashes in the ocean twinkled like heavenly sequins as they stood there, gazing at the restless waters ebbing and flowing. A long strip of white beach stretched in both directions, and the small boathouse and loading dock were the only silhouettes in the moonlight.

"It's lovely," she breathed as she watched the moving panorama of liquid sculptures made by a white-foam surf upon the sand. A cool, moist breeze touched Ashley's face, and a scent of salt and marsh grasses floated in the air.

"Yes, beautiful," he echoed, but he wasn't looking at the ocean view. When she turned to him with eyes shining as clear and beautiful as the heavens above, he couldn't drag his gaze away from her.

He saw a need in her eyes that matched his, and like a spillgate suddenly open to rushing waters, they came together in a heated embrace. He kissed her again and again, his tongue parting her lips.

Ashley let herself be carried away into a swirling maelstrom of sexual passion. Desire spiraled through her with the heat of a prairie fire, bringing sensations that threatened the control she'd always claimed. The experience was too new, too all-encompassing—and frightening! She pulled away, confused and uncertain.

Neither of them spoke for a long moment, and then Kyle said in a husky voice, "Why don't we take a brisk stroll on the beach?"

Walking along the water's edge always helped him get a clear head, and he knew that he'd never needed a clearer head more than he did at this moment: he was dangerously close to letting his heart overrule his good sense.

Ashley hesitated. She was tempted to delay returning to the house as long as possible, but on another level she knew that staying in his company was terribly filled with land mines. If he took her in his arms and kissed her again, the whole impersonation charade could come tumbling out. Even if he promised secrecy, what kind of position would that put him in with his boss? He would have to make a choice, either become a conspirator or reveal that the children's nanny was an imposter. No, it would not be fair to him to draw him into the deceit.

"I think I'll pass."

"Come on, it's a lovely night for a walk along the ocean." He needed to set things straight between them, but he didn't know how he was going to do it. He tried to put his arm around her, but she moved away.

"You don't want to go back to that boring social chitchat, do you?" he chided, trying to buy time to get some defensive strategy in place, even though he knew with dead certainty that nothing he could do or say was going to change a damn thing.

"I think I'd best make my apologies to Hugo and call it an evening. Maybe we can take a walk another time," she said. *If there is another time after my talk with Hugo tomorrow.* She was afraid that any romantic walk along the water would only invite more dangerous intimacy.

Ashley avoided his eyes as they turned back toward the house. How was she going to explain all of this to Jill?

When Kyle got back to his cottage, he found Rudy slouched down on the couch, drinking a beer and watching television. The ugly man just grunted to let Kyle know he didn't want to be interrupted. When the next commercial came on, he took a swig of his beer, and then gave Kyle a deprecating glare.

When he didn't say anything, Kyle asked, totally convinced that Rudy had been wasting his time, "Well, how did it go? Did you find anything?"

"Hell, yes." Rudy gave him a taunting broad-toothed smile. "You really dropped the ball on this one. It's a good thing the boss sent me around to keep the operation on track."

Kyle stiffened. Rudy could be bluffing or lying about something to make himself look good. He didn't trust the guy's word for anything, but he had to work with him, so he gave Rudy a puzzled look. "Really?"

"She played you for a fool, all right," Rudy sneered.

Kyle struggled to hold his temper against the man's jibes. He wanted to knock the smirk off his face. "What'd you pick up?"

"Look at this."

Kyle stared in disbelief. Rudy held a small gray cell phone in his bony hand. The one Kyle had sabotaged with glue had been black. "Where'd you find that?"

"In her room."

"Another phone?"

Rudy gave an ugly laugh. "She had two of them. You found one and quit looking, didn't ya?"

Kyle rankled under the truth. It had never entered his mind that she might have two cell phones in her possession. Why would she? It was some kind of a fluke. He hated having to take Rudy's know-it-all smirk. "I'll be damned."

"Thought you had it all set up for her to use a bugged phone, didn't you?" Rudy jeered. "And while you've been waiting to listen in on her calls, I'm betting that she's been using this one. Hell, she outsmarted ya good."

Kyle's hands clenched. He shouldn't have let the matter slide. When she didn't make any calls on the bugged phones, he should have made a second search of the room. But he hadn't. He'd accepted her at face value, and now there would be hell to pay. Rudy was right. She'd played him for a fool. *In more ways than one.* He mentally winced thinking about the heated embrace and kisses that had driven everything else from his mind.

"Wanna bet she's been calling someone as regular as a chicken lays eggs? What about that little fiasco at the lighthouse? Maybe that was a planned meeting that went wrong. You rescued the lady in distress before her ever-loving husband got there to whisk her away."

"Use your head, Rudy. She'd never leave the baby."

He snorted. "If she's as two-faced as her husband, no telling what she'd do. And she's a hell of a lot smarter than you've been giving her credit for. Hugo isn't going to like this one bit if she's been in touch with Budge all this time.'' Rudy leveled a pair of accusing black eyes on him. ''This could blow the whole damn plan to hell.''

''There's no reason to think she's planning anything.''

''How in the hell do you know? She could have made contact with Budge already. Hugo says that there are rumbles that he's never left the States. Some sightings have put him near the Georgia mainland. The boss wants him, and bad. Your neck is going to be in the wringer for missing that second phone,'' Rudy continued with open satisfaction. ''How we gonna know whether or not our bird is ready to fly?''

''I guess we don't.'' As Kyle fixed himself a drink, he went back over everything that had happened. Rudy could be right. Maybe the nanny's excursion to the lighthouse that day hadn't been all that innocent. She could have been checking out the cove as a rendezvous site, and inadvertently got herself in a jam when the lighthouse's floor gave way.

Kyle took a deep swig of his strong drink. Rudy was right. He'd been too damn gullible.

All evening Jill had seemed uneasy, not the least bit talkative. Preoccupied, maybe? Yes, definitely. She obviously had her mind on something beside a social gathering. After dinner she had wanted to take a walk alone in the garden, and he had insisted on going with her.

A sudden coldness sluiced through him. What had

happened between them could have been contrived. If she'd wanted to mislead him, her passionate kisses had done their job well. Never once did he suspect that she might be playing a part to throw him off the scent of a pending reunion with her husband. Angrily, Kyle finished off his Scotch and water.

Rudy snickered. "Trying to put out a fire, are ya? Just as I thought. She's been playing you like a damn yo-yo, hasn't she? You're gripping that glass tighter than a wound-up spring."

"Save it, Rudy," Kyle growled. "I don't need your stupid comments or advice."

"Well, here's one more. Better watch your step or you'll end up on Hugo's list of disposables."

ASHLEY DIDN'T DISCOVER that the phone was missing until the next morning. She had decided that it was too late to call Jill after she got back to her room, and she wasn't exactly certain how to tell her sister what had happened between her and Kyle.

Why had she let herself jeopardize everything by creating a relationship that wasn't fair to anyone? Even if she got by Hugo's sharp eyes, would Jill be able to carry on the charade with Kyle?

And how will you feel, thinking about them together?

She shoved the thought away. What good would it do to think about that now? This was her sister's life she was living, and not her own, and when she handed it back to Jill, she would have no control over whatever happened between her and Kyle.

"I guess I'd better give your mom a call," she told Davie as she gave a dangling mobile a gentle push to set the figures dancing.

At first Ashley thought she'd mislaid the cell phone. It took her several minutes of searching to realize that it was gone. After checking both purses, under both pillows and through the drawers in her dressing table, she stood in the middle of the room, looking around trying to understand why it wasn't in any of the places where she'd always kept it. Her own phone was still there but was no use this far from the Rocky Mountain region.

When Lily came into the nursery, Ashley asked, "Have you seen my cell phone anywhere?"

Lily looked blank. "I didn't know you had one."

Was she telling the truth? Ashley's earlier suspicion that Lily had gone through her things surfaced again. She didn't want to believe the girl was a thief, but who else would have any interest in taking a cell phone?

"I know I left it in the room," Ashley insisted.

Lily shrugged and gave Ashley a message that Hugo would like to see her in his den before she started working with the children. "I told Benny and Pamela to stay in their rooms until you came to get them."

Hugo wasn't going to waste any time having their little talk. Just as well, she thought. If the ax was going to fall, better to get it over with. There wasn't time to call Jill from a different phone. She'd have to get through this meeting with Hugo on her own.

"I thought I'd take the baby for an outing in his stroller this morning while it's still cool," Lily told her. "Are you going to take the kids swimming this afternoon?"

"I haven't thought that far ahead," Ashley admitted. "I thought their grandfather might have something planned to do with them today."

"Oh, I heard him tell Mrs. Borsch to make sure enough supplies were aboard the yacht for an overnight cruise. I think they're leaving after lunch. He won't be taking the children along, though. Too bad you can't go. It would be fun just to lie around in the sun, wouldn't it?" she said dreamily. "Eating and drinking and watching the gulls skim over the water. Maybe you could talk him into taking you and the children along?"

The very thought turned Ashley's stomach. She couldn't think of any torture more devastating than being confined on a boat with Hugo and his guests. Surely, he didn't have anything like that in mind?

Chapter Thirteen

Ashley's nervous knock on the den's half-open door caused it to swing wide enough that she could see into the room. Hugo was sitting behind a massive desk in a spacious room tastefully furnished in earth tones and masculine decor.

Rudy was with him.

As she stood there, plainly visible, their conversation came to an abrupt halt. Maybe it was only her own paranoia, but she had the impression they'd been talking about her.

"Come in, Jill," Hugo said crisply. A diamond ring sparkled on his little finger as he motioned to her.

Rudy slouched in a leather chair near the desk, and his beady eyes flickered over her with a sardonic glint as if he was about to enjoy this scene. Neither of the men got to their feet.

Ashley had done her best to dress as much like Jill as she could. A purple miniskirt hugged her thighs, long enough to hide the scratch, but still short enough to show a long expanse of shapely legs. A bright floral peasant blouse pulled low on her upper arms created an expansive neckline. When she moved her head, purple earrings that matched the skirt dangled beside her cheeks.

Ashley had never felt more on display in her life than she did that moment as she walked across the room. She feared the pounding of her heart could be seen in her throat. She had to make this good.

Hugo waited until she had reached his desk before he slowly rose from his chair. His attire was casual, sporty, a white shirt and slacks, but it showed impeccable good taste and an expensive price tag as well. Everything about him radiated wealth and autocratic authority. Ashley could see why his grandchildren were uneasy in his presence. His displeasure was not something that anyone with good sense would invite. She felt her own legs trembling.

"Good morning. I trust you slept well," he said with practiced politeness.

"Yes, thank you," she lied. "Lily said you wanted to see me." Ashley hoped her tone sounded neither defensive nor submissive, but confident and respectful. She was determined to ignore the hostility that Rudy's presence always created in her.

Hugo nodded and motioned to a chair a couple of feet away from the one where Rudy sat. "Yes, have a seat."

Ashley would have preferred to stand, but that was impossible. Hugo sat back down in his executive chair with no pretend smile on his lips, nor any sensual overtones in his manner. All traces of the accommodating host of the night before were absent from his sober expression. He was clearly disturbed about something.

She felt Rudy's eyes on her as she sat down and tucked her short skirt in as firmly as modesty would allow.

No one spoke. Hugo moved some papers on his desk as if to punctate some unpleasantness that was about to rock the room. They must know. She swallowed back a taste of bitter bile in her throat. It was all over. Where was Kyle? Why wasn't he here to add his accusations to the others? In a way, her deceit toward him had been greater than to anyone else. How could she face him now?

She almost got up and left the room, but at that moment Hugo spoke, not to her but to Rudy. "Double-check with Mrs. Borsch about provisions for the yacht. And then take the van and see to it that all the guests have transportation to the club. I want everyone there so we can leave right after lunch." He gave a dismissing wave of his hand. "That's all."

Rudy's eyes narrowed. As he pushed up from the chair and started to leave the room, his gaze bored into Ashley's face like a heated brand. His fiery anger spewed across the room at her, and she knew that he was dying to say something rude to her. She'd never seen such raw animosity in anyone's face before, and unconsciously, she shrank back in her own chair.

"That's all, Rudy," Hugo repeated in an icy tone

that warned the man to leave the room. "And close the door after you."

The order was a simple one, but it sounded ominous. Ashley wondered if her legs would even hold her if she stood up and tried to make her exit before Hugo could demand to know why she had played him for a fool.

"Unpleasant man, isn't he?" Hugo said, as the door closed behind Rudy.

For a moment, Ashley was too surprised to answer. Then she nodded. "Yes. Very."

Hugo stood up, came around the desk and surprised her by casually sitting on the corner and swinging one leg slightly as he stared down at her. She knew that any chance to run away was gone.

"I have to say that I'm disappointed in you, Jill."

Jill? He was still calling her Jill?

Ashley was so startled that all she could do was swallow hard and croak, "Disappointed? Why are you disappointed?"

He smiled then, but it was not a nice smile. "You really didn't think anything could go on in this house without my knowing it, did you, Jill?"

He still thought she was her twin.

Her relief was short-lived. Where on earth was the conversation going? Certainly not in the direction she had expected. Then the thought hit her. He must be suspicious about her and Kyle. She was trying to find some way to explain when his next words told her she was on the wrong track.

"The walls have ears, you know."

Walls? Ears? What was the man talking about? Nothing had gone on between her and Kyle inside the house. All their romantic intimacy had been outside in the garden and by the lily pond. Had Rudy been feeding Hugo a bunch of garbage? She didn't think Kyle was responsible for any suggestions that they'd been intimate. Is that what Hugo was hinting at? She didn't have the least idea how she was going to handle such veiled accusations.

"I don't know what you're talking about," she said with spirit, and gave her head a slight toss the way Jill did when she was impatient with someone.

Hugo's voice was as cold as chipped ice. "I'm told that you've been in contact with your husband. Talking to him on the phone."

Ashley blinked. *Husband?* Her brain suddenly wouldn't compute.

"Is it true, Jill?" Hugo leaned toward her. "Tell me the truth! Has Budge called you?"

Not me. Maybe Jill.

For an instant Ashley wondered if she'd spoken aloud, but Hugo's eyes hadn't changed. They were still like gray-blue grappling hooks pulling at her, demanding an answer. "You've been talking to him, haven't you?"

"Where did you get such an idea?" Ashley managed what she hoped was a wry laugh. "Everyone knows Budge is long gone. He fled with the money, left me and the baby as if we were excess baggage. Why on earth would he contact me—*Jill*—now?"

"I don't know."

"Neither do I," she said flatly. As he steadily weighed her expression, she kept her eyes firmly locked on his. "Somebody has a great imagination."

He was silent for a moment, and then he nodded, "So it would seem." Then he reached out, took her hands, and pulled her to her feet. "I gave you this job, Jill, because I felt guilty that one of my team members had played so dirty with all of us. We were both deceived and hurt by Budge. I wanted to try and make it up to you somehow."

He gave her that suggestive sensual smile, and she wanted to take a step backwards, but she was pinned between him and her chair. What was he leading up to? Was he going to exact some kind of payment for his benevolence?

"I appreciate the job," she said as evenly as she could. Nothing in the world was important enough for her to be humiliated by a cheap advance or demand from this man.

He suddenly cupped her chin with one of his mammoth hands, and studied her face. A slight frown furrowed his broad forehead. She stopped breathing. Was there some detail about her features that was giving her away?

"You're different, Jill," he said quietly, his gray eyes narrowing. "I can't quite put my finger on it. I guess motherhood has changed you."

"Yes, I guess so," she said with what little breath she had left. Thank goodness he'd offered an acceptable reason for the difference he saw in her.

"You have a son to think about now, don't you?"

he said, dropping his hand from her face. "You wouldn't do anything to jeopardize his chances of growing up well and strong, would you?"

She stiffened as she dragged her gaze away from those steely eyes. Was she being paranoid to think there was some meaning or threat behind his words?

She felt a sudden chill and suppressed a shiver as she said, "I want to do what's best for Davie, of course. I'm grateful that you are allowing me to keep him here this summer with Benny and Pamela. Everyone knows how generous you are."

She thought his eyes narrowed slightly, but he moved away from her and waved his hand toward the door. "Well, I won't keep you any longer, Jill. My staff will keep in touch with me, and I'm sure that Kyle and Rudy will be happy to see to your needs— whatever they might be."

He had said nothing to indicate that he'd found her wanting in any way, and yet she left the room with a feeling that she'd been analyzed, measured and put under some kind of a microscope.

What had he been looking for?

He clearly lacked any interest in her role as a nanny to his grandchildren—not one question about their welfare. His questions about Budge had taken her completely by surprise. Where had he picked up the idea that Jill's husband might have been in contact with her?

Instead of going back upstairs, Ashley headed for the library where there was a phone that she could use in private. Although she was relieved that the session with Hugo was over, she couldn't ignore a nagging intuition that she'd missed something.

She glimpsed Kyle just outside on the terrace and quickly shut the library doors behind her, hoping that he hadn't seen her. This might be her only chance to call her sister in private. She sat down at a library desk and dialed her twin.

After leaving the arranged message on the answering machine, she hung up and dialed again.

Jill picked up the phone almost immediately.

"Hi, it's me," Ashley said.

"Why didn't you call last night, Ashley? I waited on pins and needles. How did things go with Hugo? Did he suspect anything?"

"I don't think so. Everything seems under control, Jill. He seems to have accepted the switch without any problem. He says I'm different, but he thinks motherhood is responsible. But something has happened between Kyle Stone and me that may be a problem."

"Oh, no, Ashley. Tell me you haven't slept with him."

"I haven't, but...but things have gotten a little out of hand," she said as evenly as she could, closing her eyes and remembering the passionate kisses and sexual hunger that she'd experienced in his arms. How could she tell her sister that she'd fallen in love with a man who would never know who she was? How could she explain this torturous sense of loss to her sister, when she didn't understand it herself?

"For heaven's sake, Ashley, aren't things complicated enough without you going off the deep end for some guy? What have you set me up for? A clandestine affair with Hugo's hired hand?''

In her mind's eye, Ashley saw Jill in Kyle's arms, teasing and laughing with him, lifting her face to those questing lips of his. The vision brought a flare of anger deep within Ashley. ''If you want me to tell him the truth about all of this, I will,'' she said sharply.

''No, no, I'll handle it,'' Jill said quickly.

''I want out of this now, Jill,'' Ashley said sharply. ''Hugo's going to be gone for a few days on his yacht. This would be a good time for us to make the exchange. You sound well enough to take over.''

''I'm having a doctor's check-up tomorrow. If my lungs are clear, I can leave the next day.''

''Great. By the way, Hugo asked me if I'd been in touch with my husband.''

''What? In touch with Budge? Why would he think that?''

''Have you been in touch with Budge and not told me?''

''No, of course not.'' Jill fell silent for a moment. ''If Budge does try to contact me, it will be there on the island. He hasn't, has he?''

''Of course not.'' Ashley dismissed the idea as wishful thinking on Jill's part.

''Do you think it could be true, Ashley? Do you think Budge would really risk his neck coming back for me?'' A lift of hopefulness was evident in her voice.

"No, I think he's long gone," Ashley said flatly. "And you'd be a fool to try and take up with him if he did appear. He's a fugitive, for pity's sake, Jill. What kind of a life would you have running from the law morning, noon and night?"

"I guess you're right." Jill sighed. "Sometimes, I feel guilty, wondering if maybe Budge stole the money because we used to fantasize about what fun we'd have if we suddenly had a million dollars. I guess being with wealthy people like Hugo turned our heads a little."

Ashley didn't argue with her. It was true. Her sister always talked about wanting to be one of the jet set who enjoyed expensive clothes and world travel.

" I can't believe I'm going to be living in the Vandenburg mansion all summer," Jill said with awe in her voice.

"Better you than me," Ashley said dryly, and they both laughed.

KYLE FELT as if someone had given him a double punch in the stomach as he sat listening to the conversation on the library's bugged phone. He couldn't believe what he was hearing.

When he'd seen Ashley slip into the library, he'd quickly hurried back to the cottage just in time to see the red light on his bugging equipment come on. He could have listened to the recorded conversation later, but he grabbed a set of earphones—impatient to know who she'd been calling on that second cell phone.

At first, he was taken aback that it was a woman

she had phoned. After spending the night thinking about it, he had been convinced that she'd been using the cell to contact her fugitive husband. He'd barely had time to adjust his thinking before he was nearly knocked off his chair by the verbal exchange that assaulted his ears.

Everything seems under control, Jill. Hugo seems to have accepted the switch without any problem....

Kyle listened in absolute shock. Never in his life had he been hit with anything so completely unexpected—and so perilous to everyone involved. For several minutes after the conversation had stopped, he just sat there as his mind whirled.

How had it happened? Someone sure as hell had dropped the ball!

He took out the tape of the recorded phone call and put in a new one. Rudy would be snooping around, checking on the tapes and Kyle didn't want him to tumble onto the truth that the woman they had been guarding wasn't Jill Gordon at all. He wanted to do some checking of his own.

His expression was grim as he used his own cell to call a private number. He then gave a password—*Warrior*—to his contact in the FBI. He'd been an active undercover agent for the last five years, handling some difficult cases. He was known as a fighter, hence the password.

"Hi, Kyle," Sorenson answered. "How's Operation Vandenburg going?"

"The bottom just fell out of it!" Kyle's temper

flared. "I risk my neck going undercover and someone doesn't even check out the pigeon!"

"What are you talking about?"

"I'm talking about Jill Gordon and the fact that she has an identical twin and nobody checked it out! The report I had on her only listed a sister in Colorado who is a college professor. That was it! There wasn't a hint that the sister was an identical twin named Ashley! Guess what?"

"Don't tell me," Sorenson pleaded.

"You got it! They pulled a switch on us."

His boss swore. "I'll be damned."

"I don't think Budge knows about their switch," Kyle added after filling Sorenson in on the reason for the switch. "From their bugged conversation, it doesn't sound as if either of them have been in contact with him."

"Good, then maybe we can keep the operation in place."

"Let's hope so. Hugo's got a network of informants all over the place trying to pick up Budge's trail. He's positive that the guy hasn't left the country. Word is that Budge is somewhere in the vicinity."

"Hell, if Vandenburg gets his hands on him before we do, this whole operation will turn out to be one fat goose egg," Sorenson warned. "Without Gordon's testimony, we'll never be able to tie Vandenburg to the illegal betting scam. Our only hope is to grab Gordon and promise a plea bargain if he'll testify against the team owner."

Kyle fumed silently. Sorenson didn't need to tell

him what was at stake. Not only could the operation blow up in their faces, but this kind of mishandling of his tenuous undercover deception could threaten his own safety. Hugo didn't play lightly when it came to weeding out traitors in his organization.

"How soon do you think Jill Gordon will switch places with her twin?" Sorenson demanded.

"Jill's having a physical tomorrow. If she's okay, it'll only be a couple of days before they make the switch." Not only did it rankle Kyle that he'd been deceived, but this Ashley gal must have been gloating all the time.

"Well, then, no real harm done," Sorenson said, letting out an audible breath. "Nobody else knows about this, do they? She's fooled everyone?"

Kyle's response was curt. "She damn well fooled me."

"What about Vandenburg? He knows Jill Gordon personally. Even if the twin is identical, there are bound to be some differences in manner and attitude."

"As far as I know Hugo seems satisfied that he has Jill Gordon under wraps. At least, Ashley—that's her name—told Jill that Hugo has bought the switch. I'm worried about Rudy Dietz, though. If that miserable guy catches a whiff of this, all hell's likely to break loose. Both women could be in danger."

"You've got to keep the lid on and let this thing play out. Our men are in place and ready to move whenever you give the word. We've got to get to Gordon first."

"I know. Rudy told me that Hugo's got men all over the island just waiting for the word that Budge has been spotted. Rudy's pushing for control. He'll try to cut me out if he can."

"Don't let that happen. We've got to get to Gordon first. And, Kyle don't get in the way of the twins making the switch."

"Don't worry, I'll play dumb," he said gruffly, chafing at the idea that he'd have to deliberately look the other way while the two of them were playing out their deception.

"The sooner we have the real Jill on the premises, the better chance this thing will fly the way we want it to," his boss said. "Sounds as if all you have to do is hold steady for a few days."

"No problem," he answered wryly. All he had to do was keep relating to Ashley in a way that wouldn't arouse her suspicions that he knew she was playing him for a perfect dunce.

In his heart, he knew that this might just turn out to be the hardest challenge of his life.

Chapter Fourteen

Ashley and the children were heading for the beach when Kyle ran to catch up with them. He was in swimming trunks and a short terrycloth robe and had a towel thrown over his shoulder.

"Great weather for a morning swim. Here, let me help," he said, taking the beach ball from Benny who was struggling to hold it along with his snorkel gear.

"I thought you were busy with Hugo and his guests at the Yacht Club," she said as he fell into step beside her.

"Nope, Rudy's taking care of the gophering." He gave Ashley a broad smile that he hoped would mask his feeling. "How did your meeting go with Hugo this morning?" he asked deliberately, unable to resist the temptation to put her on the hot seat. He'd heard her tell Jill that she'd pulled it off, and he knew that playing out her role in front of the boss must have been a challenge. There was no denying her art of deception.

God knows, she hadn't been honest with him from

the moment he saw her. How she must have been laughing at him all this time. Not only had she jeopardized months of tedious work to infiltrate Hugo's subversive activities, but she'd played havoc with his feelings for her.

"He didn't ask me anything about the children," she said softly so that Pamela and Benny couldn't hear.

Her answer took him aback for a moment. She seemed sincerely disturbed about Hugo's lack of interest in his grandchildren. As he thought back about her enthusiastic interest in the books the kids had made and the way she'd used the house tour to stimulate their interest in pictures and art objects, he realized that she'd never really been the kind of woman that had been reported to him.

Of course not, Ashley Camdon was a college professor.

Kyle silently swore at himself. What a dunce he'd been, accepting her at face value. The heavy makeup and trendy clothes had fooled him completely. Even the skimpy swimming suit and sheer overblouse that she was wearing now were all part of the disguise. Several times he'd had fleeting glimpses that didn't fit her looks or reputation, but he had ignored his intuitive sense that something was out of focus.

"I don't think Hugo's ever been really paternal," Kyle answered smoothly. "Don't worry about it. I'm sure you've succeeded in convincing him that the children are in good hands."

"I hope so," she said with little conviction.

He wondered if she was worried about her sister taking over the nanny job. There was no discounting the perception of children. Benny and Pamela might very well notice the difference.

"We're playing hookey this morning," Benny told him, grinning. "Jilly said we could."

"Good idea." He wasn't surprised that she wasn't in the mood to spend the morning in the library after her meeting with Hugo.

"I'm going to take my afternoon off today," she told him. "I thought it was a good idea for the children to spend the morning at the beach since Lily said they'd be watching television or playing quietly in their rooms most of the afternoon."

"And how are you going to spend your well-deserved time off?" he asked as casually as he could.

"I haven't decided yet."

When they reached the stretch of beach near the boathouse, the children dropped their towels and started to rush toward the water.

"Wait up! Not until you get some sunscreen on you."

Ashley sat down on the sand, opened her beach bag, and, ignoring the children's impatient wiggles, she applied a generous coat of lotion to their brown little bodies. "Okay. Now stay where I can see you. And no snorkeling in water above your waist, Benny."

"Sure thing!" he agreed happily.

She laughed as they bounded off, squealing when

they splashed into the surf and threw themselves into the water.

"Aren't you going to join them?" Kyle asked, standing above her, trying to ignore her beautiful proportions as she leaned back on her arms and looked up at him. He was painfully aware of her delicate features framed by hair set on fire by the sun. The rise and fall of her breath accented the fullness of tantalizing breasts barely concealed by the scanty bathing bra. Knowing that she wasn't married released a floodgate of emotions and desires that he no longer had to hold back.

"I thought I'd catch a little sun first." Avoiding his eyes, she took off the sheer blouse, uncapped the sunscreen bottle and began applying the lotion to her face, midriff, arms and legs.

She was a real siren, all right. Any man would have to be dead and buried not to be unnerved by the way her supple body invited a lover's touch, he thought as he dropped down beside her.

"Want some lotion?" she offered politely.

He shook his head, and, sitting with his arms around his pulled-up legs, he fixed his gaze on the romping children and the passage of several sailboats, cabin cruisers and even a cruise ship far off on the horizon. It was a scene he loved, but all his senses were filled with the awareness of her lovely body sitting beside him. This might be the last time that they would be alone like this, he thought with a surprising sense of loss. Never in his career with the FBI had he wanted to walk out on an assignment as much as he did this one.

For one crazy moment, he thought about leveling with her, telling her the real reason that Jill Gordon had been given the nanny job. What would she do if she knew the truth? he asked himself, but even as the question passed his mind, he knew the answer.

She'd keep her sister as far away from here as possible.

The whole success of his undercover mission depended upon her continuing the deception until the real Jill arrived. If Ashley caught a whiff of the truth that her twin was being manipulated, she'd make sure that Jill never set foot on this island. The necessity to play along with her double-dealing stuck in his craw, but there was nothing he could do about it.

Pushing to his feet, he stood over her. "Time to hit the water."

Ashley was startled by the angry edge of his tone. Without waiting for agreement, he reached down with one hand and pulled her to her feet. She wanted to protest the man-handling. He was looking at her strangely, as if peeling away layers, trying to find the core of her being.

"What is it?" she asked in a tight voice. The firm, hard stance of his lean body brought a rush of remembered desire, and for a moment he seemed to waver toward her.

At that moment the children came bounding back, squealing, "We saw a dolphin. We saw a dolphin. Come on...come on." Excitedly, they pointed to an outcrop that extended into the water. "He's playing just off the rocks over there."

Ashley dragged her eyes from Kyle's mesmerizing face as the children danced around them.

"Let's go see it," Benny urged. "Maybe it's Flipper."

"That's only a movie," Pamela said with the disgust of an older sister.

Benny pulled at Ashley's hand. "Hurry. Hurry."

Relieved to get away from Kyle and the unspoken tension between them, she said, "Okay. Let's go take a look."

Leaving the towels, ball and beach bag where they had dropped them, they followed Benny as he bounded ahead of them, urging them to hurry.

"I didn't know there were any dolphins around here," Ashley said as her gaze traveled over slightly ruffled blue-green water, hoping that the children hadn't mistaken a floating piece of driftwood for a playful dolphin.

Kyle shrugged. "I think I heard someone at the Yacht Club say that sometimes you could glimpse them through the windows in the dining room. I didn't know they strayed down the beach this far."

They had to walk quite a distance before they reached a natural rock-and-dirt pier that extended out into the water. Ashley and Kyle stayed close to the children in case they missed their footing on the rocky outcropping.

Very quietly, they all sat down, and waited patiently as the water splashed against the rocks. They searched the surrounding waters for some glimpse of a tail or an arched body leaping through the surf.

Nothing.

Benny began to grumble impatiently, and Ashley wondered how much the boy knew about dolphins. She'd have to suggest to Jill that she follow through on his interest with some books and stories. The realization that her time with the children was almost over briefly shadowed her relief that the charade was nearly at an end.

She let her gaze touch Kyle's face for a brief moment, and, sitting there with him and the children, she suddenly knew that everything she'd been through had been worth this one moment. Even though the dolphin never appeared, Ashley was grateful that the children had given her this contented memory to take with her.

Benny was vocal in his disappointment as they carefully made their way back over the rocky barrier. "Can't we swim here, in case he comes back?" he begged, unwilling to give up on his hope of seeing Flipper again.

"I don't see why not," Kyle answered, eyeing the sandy beach. "I'll go back and get the towels and stuff. Okay, Jill?"

The name almost stuck in his throat as he said it, but he had to keep thinking of her as Jill and not Ashley. It wasn't easy, but when her twin arrived it was going to be even harder to pretend he'd been duped by the switch.

She nodded. "I'll swim with the kids while you're

gone. If the dolphin is around, maybe he'll want to come play with us.'' She knew she was just spinning a fantasy for Benny, but what was life without a few fantasies?

As the three of them splashed into the surf, Kyle hiked down the beach back to where they had dropped their stuff. In order to carry everything more easily, he opened the beach bag to put the suntan lotion, goggles and a couple of towels inside.

That's when he saw the note. Right on top. It wasn't even folded, and he didn't even have to lift it out to read it.

> Jill, darling, I love you. I want you with me. If you feel the same, bring the baby and signal me with a flashlight from the boat ramp and I'll pick you up.
>
> Tomorrow night, twelve o'clock. Don't tell anyone! B

Kyle swore. This was exactly what both Hugo and the FBI had been waiting for. Budge was making good the promise he'd made to his wife in the letter Hugo had confiscated. There was only one hitch. They had the wrong woman in place.

Kyle clenched his fist angrily. He couldn't believe that Budge had been here on the beach right under his nose. Somehow the fugitive had managed to put the note in the beach bag without being seen. Even though Kyle realized that the beach curved enough so this section wasn't visible from where he'd been sitting, he still was furious with himself.

Kyle began searching for telltale footprints in the sand, and found some leading away from the beach bag in a straight line to the nearby boat dock. Now he knew what had happened. Budge must have been on one of those boats that had been cruising offshore. With a strong pair of binoculars he could have followed them as they walked down the beach to the rock outcropping. While they sat there waiting to see the dolphin, he was able to dock the boat for the brief time that it took him to leave the note. Somehow he'd even managed to escape notice from any of Hugo's men.

Kyle searched the rolling waters in every direction as far as his eyes could see. Only a couple of shrimp trawlers were in sight now. Even the sailboats had disappeared. No sign of a small boat anywhere on the glittering water.

Thoughtfully, he turned and walked back to the open beach bag. What would Jill's twin do when she found the note? Should he leave it? Or take it? For a long moment, he tried to play both scenarios in his mind. He decided to keep it. He needed time to analyze the situation from every angle. Whatever he did now could spell success or failure for the FBI's elaborate undercover operation.

Ashley and the children were still in the water when he walked back to them. They waved and shouted for him to join them, and he forced himself to behave as normally as he could while he decided what to do next.

"Will you watch them?" Ashley called to him as he played with the two children in the water. "I'm going to swim out to the buoy and back."

He nodded and watched her lithe body cut through the water with the grace of a mermaid. Clean and swift strokes covered the distance easily, and when she returned to the beach, her breathing was only slightly fast.

"Good swimming." He smiled approvingly as she sat down on a towel beside him and began drying herself. Obviously, she loved the water and was a strong swimmer. He wished he knew more about her, not only to judge what she might do in this hazardous situation, but because an irrational part of him couldn't dismiss the powerful effect she had on him.

LUNCH WAS a quick affair. Mrs. Borsch, Gerta and the extra help were out of sorts. The aftermath of preparing for and cleaning up after Hugo's house-guests had taken its toll on all the staff. Lily was happy that she could spend the afternoon tending Davie and keeping an eye on Benny and Pamela instead of helping with the housework. Ashley was relieved that Rudy still hadn't returned from the Yacht Club so they were spared his company.

Kyle had invited Ashley to go shopping with him. He was hoping that spending the afternoon with Ashley would help him come to some decision about what to do about the note. He'd tried to get in touch with Sorenson, but he'd been out of the office and hadn't called him back.

As they left the house in Kyle's red Jaguar, he could tell from the way Ashley sat stiffly in the seat and the way her hands kept fingering the strap on her white purse that her thoughts were on something more than just the anticipation of a relaxing afternoon off. A simple white tunic dress hugged her figure and the view of her long legs revealed by the short skirt did nothing to settle his turbulent thoughts.

No matter how much he would hate himself for manipulating her, he had no choice. Once he talked to Sorenson, he would have to carry out orders. He didn't see how either of them could get out of this double deception without destroying everything soft and tender that had been between them.

"Is something the matter?" Kyle asked quietly, hoping that the open-ended question might give him more of an insight into the woman she really was. Even though they both were wearing masks and hiding their true identities, he knew that in some almost miraculous way he had connected with her and she with him.

She forced herself to respond lightly. "Maybe just a little tired from the morning's swim."

He nodded, but he knew that it wasn't a physical tiredness that she was carrying around, but the heavy burden of deceit. He was fighting the same tiredness himself.

When they reached the small business district, they left the car in a public lot and walked along the waterfront. A ferry from the mainland had just docked and Ashley quickly looked at her watch. One-fifteen. That might be the best one for Jill to take. Ashley's thoughts skipped ahead to the logistics of exchanging cars and clothes. She was so engrossed in her own thoughts that she didn't realize for a moment that Kyle was waiting for an answer to something he'd said.

"I'm sorry, I was…daydreaming."

"I was suggesting that we could arrange to meet in an hour. Would that give you enough time to do your shopping?"

"Perfect," she said, relieved that he was offering her the time to go off by herself.

"Good." Kyle wanted to give her a long leash. Whatever she did now could be vital in handling the situation. "Shall we meet here?" They were standing near a marina, filled with private boats. "My friend has a cruiser that I borrow sometimes. It's that white one with the blue trim. I'll say hello to him while I'm waiting for you. Can you find your way back there?"

She nodded. "About an hour?"

"Fine." He watched her walk away and then nodded to a small man in a gray shirt and dark pants who was lounging against a post watching a pair of pelicans dive for fish.

As Ashley passed him, the man waited for a moment, then turned away from the water and casually followed her down the walk.

Kyle smiled in satisfaction. Joe Belin was as good as one could get when it came to trailing someone.

Wherever Ashley went and whatever she said, he'd be close enough to see and hear everything.

Kyle hurried down the marina steps and boarded the government's "safe" boat that was kept in readiness. He wanted to call Sorenson again and deliver the bad news.

ASHLEY WALKED briskly along the seafront, weaving her way through the crowd of people and cars pouring off the ferry. She passed all the tourist shops without giving them a glance and made her way to the Waterfront Hotel. Once inside, she made her way across the lobby to a bank of public telephones and dialed Jill's number.

"How did it go, Jill? What did the doctor say?" Ashley held her breath.

"The check-up went great! I need a day to get ready, and then I'll be on my way."

"Great. I'll meet you at the mainland ferry. You'll have to start early, Jill, so we'll have time to make the switch right after lunch."

"That early?"

"Listen, Jill, you have to get back to the house before dinner."

"Ashley, I was thinking more like three or four o'clock," Jill said, sounding exasperated.

"You don't understand, Jill. The house runs on a schedule. You can't come and go as you please."

"Okay," she said, obviously resigned. "Call me tomorrow night and we'll go over everything. Is Davie okay? I can hardly wait to see him."

"He's fine. You just get here without any more delays, okay?"

Ashley hung up the receiver and turned away from the phone. Tears edged into the corner of her eyes, she didn't know why. Only one more day and the masquerade would be over. She should be singing and congratulating herself on a job well done. Once more she'd rescued her sister. But this time, Ashley knew that the price had been one that she would continue to pay for the rest of life. The man who had captured her heart and touched her on the deepest level would be a part of her memory forever. She would lie to Jill about her feelings for Kyle Stone, and in the end, maybe that would help her lie to herself.

She walked across the lobby, and then did something that was completely out of character. She went into a bar in the middle of the afternoon and ordered a drink. A farewell drink—Sex on the Beach.

The hour was almost over when she hastily bought a couple of tourist curios to prove to her friends that she'd been vacationing, and then headed back toward the marina.

KYLE HAD BEEN WAITING on the bow of the cruiser for Ashley when the small vibrating pager went off in his pocket.

Sorenson! Kyle hurried down into the cabin and returned the call.

"We've got trouble," Kyle said without any preliminaries, and proceeded to tell him about the note. He explained how the whole thing had happened.

"Budge must have pulled into the boat dock, left the note and taken off again. He wants to meet his wife tomorrow night—only we haven't got his wife! As you know, we've got her sister."

There was a moment of weighed silence, and then Sorenson said briskly, "Then she'll have to play the part."

Kyle stiffened. "Why would she?"

"You'll have to convince her to do it."

"Convince her? *How* in heaven's name?

"Just explain what's at stake."

"You mean lie to her about the danger? Convince her that there's no chance of her getting hurt?"

"What's the matter with you? You know how long and hard we've been working to nail Vandenburg. For years, he's been fleecing the sports world to line his own pockets and now we have a chance to get him. If we wait, the bastard will get to Gordon first and shut his mouth—permanently."

"I want to see Hugo behind bars as much as the next guy," Kyle snapped.

"I know you do," his boss responded smoothly. "But there's no telling how long it will be before Budge tries to contact his wife again—if he ever does. We can't let this opportunity get by us. We'll move in on him before he has a chance to know anything. Just have this look-alike on that beach at midnight. I'll have our men in place, ready to move. You've been damn lucky to stay undercover this long without someone tumbling to a mole in Vandenburg's operation."

"Using Jill Gordon to trap Budge without her knowledge is one thing. But if we send Ashley in there, and Budge tumbles to the truth that she's not his wife, he could retaliate!"

At that moment, Kyle looked up and went as cold as an iceberg.

Ashley was standing in the doorway of the cabin. Her stunned expression told him she'd overheard his end of the conversation.

"I'll call you back," he told Sorenson and broke the connection. Very deliberately he put the cell phone back in his pocket, took a deep breath and tried to force some moisture into his dry mouth.

"Come in, Ashley. We need to talk."

Chapter Fifteen

He knew.... He called her Ashley. All this time he must have been playing up to her, pretending to accept her as Jill. Ashley dropped down on a cabin sofa, numb and stunned. Her thoughts were in such a whirlwind that she scarcely heard Kyle talking to someone on deck. An engine began to hum and the boat began to move. On some detached level she knew that they were moving out of the harbor.

She pressed her fingers against her temples. None of it made sense. She was like a fly caught in a tangled mesh.

Jill, Jill, what have we done? Had her sister been honest with her? And what part had Kyle been playing in this whole scenario? What should she do?

She willed herself to think, to get a grip and ignore the perspiration beading on her brow. Suddenly her breath caught. Where was he taking the boat? She'd been a fool not to leave immediately instead of sitting here, waiting for him to explain everything.

As she came out of the cabin door, she saw that they were heading north, out to sea.

"Stop. Turn back," she shouted above the roar of wind and water, and grabbed his arm as he stood at the wheel.

He shook his head and scanned the wide expanse of ocean. Only a distant sailboat was visible heading back toward the island. They were far enough out to sea to avoid most pleasure traffic.

As he killed the engine and dropped the heavy anchor, he said, "I just wanted to get away from prying eyes. Let's go below." He put a guiding hand on her arm, but she pulled away.

"Take me back!"

"Not until we talk, Ashley."

She glared at him. "All right. We'll talk." Straightening her shoulders, and brushing away the hair blowing across her face, she said, "Then you'll take me back."

"Agreed."

Ashley sat down stiffly on the sofa, and Kyle remained standing for a long moment looking down at her. He knew she was reeling as if she'd taken a hard punch to the stomach. Everything about her assaulted his deepest feelings for her. If he'd had a choice, he would have eased down beside her, and taken her in his arms. Instead he dropped down in a nearby chair, trying to focus on what needed to be said—and in the right sequence.

"How could you have known all this time...and

let me go on pretending to be Jill?'' she demanded before he could say anything.

"I've only known since you made the call this morning in the library. We've had the house phone bugged." He gave her a wry smile. "You threw us a curve, having two cell phones, or I'd have been on to the deception after that first night you called your twin."

Ashley blinked. "Why did you want to monitor my…Jill's…telephone calls?"

"We suspected that Budge would try to get in contact with her because of a letter we intercepted."

"Who's 'we'?"

His eyes narrowed, and he leaned forward so that he could look her directly in the face. "You're going to be holding a live grenade in your hands when I answer that. I pray to God that I haven't made a mistake about your integrity."

His intensity frightened her. "Maybe I don't want to know."

He sighed. "That's the problem. You have to know. You have to know everything." He wished that there had been time to relate to her as the person she really was. He had glimpsed depths of her character, but in many respects she was still a mystery to him.

As he began to talk, she listened to him like someone caught in a scenario of the impossible. Even as his lips moved, she had difficulty comprehending the words coming from his mouth.

"My real name is Kyle Lawrence. I'm an undercover agent for the Federal Bureau of Investigation, and I took the identity of a man named Stone so I could infiltrate Hugo Vandenburg's illegal betting organization. The real Stone is in protective custody. Hugo doesn't know that. Because Stone was so deeply in trouble with the law, Hugo felt secure hiring him when I showed up.''

''He murdered someone, didn't he? That's why Lily heard the rumor about you.''

Kyle nodded. ''Rudy was probably the one spreading it. Stone's tough reputation is the only thing that keeps that creep off my neck. Rudy's like a bloodhound, sniffing for anything that might not smell right. If he knew who I really was—'' he broke off. There was no use going there. So far, he'd been able to maintain his cover.

Kyle went on to explain that even though the FBI knew that Hugo was responsible for game-fixing, they had no way to prove it. ''I was after that proof when Budge Gordon double-crossed Hugo. He won the game he was supposed to throw, and made off with the money he'd bet on winning. Hugo is not a good loser. As luck would have it, he intercepted a letter to Jill that Budge had left with another player. In it, Jill's husband declares his love and his determination to somehow come back for her.''

''So that's why he offered Jill the nanny's job,'' Ashley said with a catch in her throat.

''Exactly. Which brings us to you. No one else knows that you're not Jill Gordon.''

''It really doesn't matter, does it? Under the circumstances, I'm certainly not about to save this job for Jill.'' She took a deep breath. ''She's well out of it.''

''Not exactly, I'm afraid.'' He reached in his pocket and drew out a slip of paper. ''I found this in your beach bag this morning when I went back for the towels.''

As she read the note, an expression of dismay crept across her face. He watched her lips tighten, her eyes widen in disbelief and her fingers tremble as she stared at it. She was stunned, no doubt about it.

''Budge expects Jill to meet him tomorrow night,'' he said softly.

''Thank God she isn't here.''

''No, but you are, Ashley.''

''No, I'm through. It's over.''

Sometimes he hated what he'd sworn to do for justice. This was one of those times. He wanted to shut out the whole damn world with its ugliness and greed. But he couldn't.

Sighing, he left his chair and moved over to the couch beside her. All his efforts had been leading up to a deadly plan of action that required Ashley's co-operation. If there'd been any other way to finish the rotten business, he would have grabbed at it. But there wasn't. If Budge's wife was not on the beach tomorrow night, the bottom dropped out of the law's chances of getting him as a material witness against Hugo. Every day that passed put the basketball player in more danger of being eliminated by one of Hugo's men. He was certain that Rudy was already planning on having the honor of wiping him out.

"There's one way out of this," he said evenly. "You could switch places with Jill tomorrow and give her the note."

"No." She shook her head. "She mustn't know about the note. Jill might very well set her mind to go with him."

"We're ready for that contingency. They won't get far."

"You're asking me to betray my sister," she flared.

"No, I'm asking you to help us put an evil man behind bars," he answered evenly. "It's got to be done. Now or later. And the longer Hugo goes on, cheating people, making more and more money, the harder it's going to be to get him cornered. Innocent people have already died because of his greed. Now, we have a chance to stop him by using Budge as a prosecutor's witness."

"How do you know Budge will testify against Hugo?"

"When we arrest him, he'll be facing a long prison sentence, and Budge will be ready to plea-bargain. You can bet on it."

"I don't think I could do it." Her voice was strained. "Betray Budge like that."

His arm went around her shoulders. "God knows, I wish there was another way."

Ashley wanted to pull away from him, deny all the responses her body was making to his protective touch. As she looked into his face, she saw that his dark eyes were shadowed, and his taut cheeks and mouth betrayed an inner tightness.

He had told her the truth, and she didn't doubt for a moment that he would sacrifice his own safety for the justice he believed in. Her rational mind raced to understand him in this different context, but she realized that on some intuitive level her heart had judged him correctly all along. With surprising certainty, she knew she trusted him.

Kyle saw the surrender in her eyes, and when he brushed a kiss to her forehead, she gave in to the need to let herself rest against the warm cradle of his shoulder. Neither of them spoke as the boat rocked gently with the rhythm of the ocean. An iridescent glow came through the portholes, bathing the small cabin in a soft light. The harshness of the world suddenly seemed far away, as if they were somehow suspended in a kind, healing place.

He gently stroked her cheek with the tip of one finger. "I've been torn apart trying to deny my feelings for you."

She heard the torment in his voice and regretted that she was responsible for it. "I never expected something like this to happen. It all seemed so simple in the beginning. Just a few days playing nanny, and that would be it. I never...I never expected that... that..." she faltered.

He cupped her chin with his hand and searched her face "That we would fall in love?" The answer he saw in her luminous blue eyes brought a smile to his lips. "It's true, then?"

"Yes," she answered, knowing exactly what he was asking.

"You really love me," he said in a kind of wonderment. At her nod, he lowered his mouth to hers and his kisses eliminated the need for any more words.

As his hands and lips traced the beauty of her face, neck and breasts, he marveled that beneath her feminine loveliness was a courageous spirit, strong and giving. She responded to his kisses and caresses with a generosity that invaded all his physical senses and touched him on levels he had never known before.

Miraculously, despite the masquerade of a double deception, they had found each other. Ashley trembled in his arms, matching the rising hunger of his desire. She wanted to touch him, feel every inch of his vibrant body. A murmur of pleasure escaped from her lips. As their clothes fell away and lay in a tumbled heap beside the sofa, he gathered her to him.

Delighting in the sweetness of her breasts, thighs and legs, his hands traced the curves of her body as she lay naked in the circle of his arms. She gasped as an invading warmth filled the deepest level of her consciousness. Never had she imagined the incredible sensations that carried her away when he became one with her. She whispered in total wonderment, "I found you…I found you."

THE SUN was low on the horizon when they emerged from the cabin, and Kyle made ready to head back to the marina. A sunset of yellow, fuschia and orange spread across the water and turned clouds to gold. They stood on the deck holding each other, immersed in each other and drawn into the beauty and vastness of sky and ocean.

He kissed her lightly and then said regretfully, "We've got to get back."

"I know." She was totally aware of the masculine grace of his firm body as he turned away from her and made ready for the return trip. For a few halcyon hours, they had separated themselves from the world. As they had made love, she had discovered a passionate nature within her that had lain dormant and undiscovered—until now.

He smiled at her as the boat surged forward through the water, spilling ribbons of white wake behind them. She wanted to cling to these few hours of bliss because they might be all she would ever have. There were too many unanswered questions and the future was too uncertain to think beyond this moment. In a few minutes they would be back in port, and all the unresolved demands upon both of them would have to be answered.

He had not asked her again to meet Budge, and if he had, she wasn't sure what answer she would have given him. Now that her disguise had been discovered, she wanted to be done with Hugo Vandenburg and everything connected with him. The whole idea of being involved in the federal operation terrified her. She wanted to pack up the baby and leave now. The nanny job didn't matter any more. All of them had only wanted to use Jill as bait.

She shivered to think that she might have been the one to put her sister in such a dangerous position, and she recoiled from the idea that she was being drawn into an even deeper level of deception.

What will he do if I say no?

He caught her measuring glance. "What is it?"

"I was just wondering what you would do about Budge if I can't do what you ask."

"That's up to my boss. He'll probably put a stake-out at the beach and hope Budge will bring his boat in even if he doesn't see his wife on the boat dock, waiting for him." His mouth tightened. "Maybe that would be the best way to go, anyway. Keep you out of danger."

"But what if that plan fails?"

"Then I guess we'll just hope he tries to contact Jill again—wherever she is. One thing is sure, Hugo won't give up."

She stiffened. What was he saying? Would both the law and Hugo continue to use Jill and the baby as a lure to catch her husband? Ashley suddenly felt cold in the sea breeze and lowering sun. The euphoric bliss of the afternoon ebbed away.

They both fell silent as Kyle brought the boat into the marina and a small man who had been waiting at the dock helped berth the cruiser in its slip. Kyle said something in private to him, and then helped Ashley out of the boat and up the steps of the dock.

"Who is that?"

"A fellow who watches the boat and does odd jobs."

"I think I've seen him somewhere before."

Kyle nodded. "He was beside you when you made your call to Jill in the inn." Taking a cassette tape from his pocket, he showed it to her. "He recorded your side of the conversation."

She stared at the tape in his hand. Then she said coldly, "I see. I've been like a fish in a bowl all the time, haven't I?"

"Let's say you've challenged our surveillance more than once." He grinned at her, but she didn't return the smile.

Her eyes bit into his. "I haven't so much as burped without someone reporting it, have I?"

"I wouldn't go that far. Besides you were up to the challenge. Admit you had a few laughs on me." He ran a hand through his windblown hair. "I should have tumbled that first night when you told me you wanted a Sex on the Beach to drink at dinner. You looked uncomfortable as hell. Pretending to be your sister must have been a real challenge."

"I'm glad it's over."

"Is it?"

The question hung in the air between them. She didn't answer, and he didn't pressure her, but she noticed that he was no longer smiling.

They drove back to the house in a heavy silence, but as they pulled into the driveway in front of the house, Kyle swore. Rudy was leaning against one of the marble pillars, smoking a cigarette. Kyle could tell from his manner that he was obviously waiting for them. No doubt he'd been told to stay close to him and keep a watchful eye. Hugo had men all over the island just waiting for a signal that Budge was taking the bait.

"Careful does it," he warned Ashley. "If Rudy

guesses the truth about either of us, all hell will break loose.''

She suppressed a shiver, knowing that Kyle's life was in danger and had been all the months he'd been in Hugo's employment. He squeezed her hand and got out of the car.

Rudy stamped out his cigarette and waited for them to come up the steps. His ferret eyes dragged across their faces like grappling hooks. ''I was beginning to wonder what you two were up to.'' His ugly smile was for Ashley. ''Somebody said you went shopping, Jill. I was in the village myself, but I didn't see either of you.''

''We rented a boat and went for a harbor cruise,'' Kyle answered smoothly. He'd learned to stick to the truth as much as possible.

''Why are you so interested in what I do on my day off?'' Ashley demanded, half frightened and half angry at Rudy's over-bearing manner. She knew that Jill wouldn't have put up with his attitude for one minute.

''Oh, I wasn't looking for you. I was looking for Kyle.'' He smirked. ''But I can see that he was... busy.''

Ashley tried to maintain a noncommital expression. ''If you'll excuse me, I need to relieve Lily,'' she said shortly, and brushed by the horrid man.

As she hurried up the stairs, her heart was racing. Would Kyle be able to handle the situation? What if Rudy knew they were lovers? What if—? *Stop it!* She drew in a shaky breath as she paused outside the nursery door. Even as she fought an overwhelming urge to leave the house that minute, she knew that she couldn't go. Running away would only put Jill under constant surveillance, or end up getting Budge killed if Hugo's men got to him first. And what about Kyle? His life would be in jeopardy if anyone suspected his true identity.

She had no choice. Tomorrow night, she would have to be on the beach just as Kyle wanted.

NERVOUS SWEAT beaded on Kyle's brow. It was almost twelve o'clock. Where was Ashley? She should have been here by now. Had they taken care of all the possible contingencies that could foul up the plan? Rudy was asleep on the cottage sofa, knocked out by a drugged drink that Kyle had fixed for him earlier that evening when he dropped by to harass him. Kyle had contacted Sorenson who had assured him that all the government boats and agents were in place to move in once they saw Budge's boat come to shore.

Ever the young romantic, Lily had readily agreed to watch the baby when Ashley told her she had a late date with Kyle. They had managed to get one of Pamela's baby dolls to put in the infant carrier, and they had a flashlight to signal Budge as the note had instructed.

What had they forgotten?

The night was warm and sultry with a reluctant moon half-hidden by huge whale-like clouds floating across the sky. Kyle would have preferred a brighter, clearer view of the beach and ocean waters as they flowed in dark ripples toward the land. Hiding in a mound of rocks slanting down to the white stretch, he could only see shadowy lines and angles of the boathouse and small dock. He knew he wouldn't be able to spy a boat coming in but government boats scattered about in the vastness of the nearby waters would be aware of its arrival and move in.

Kyle was about to leave his position and go look for Ashley when he glimpsed her shadowy figure moving slowly along the edge of the water toward the boat dock. Thank God. So far so good.

Ashley's steps grew slower the closer she came to the boathouse and dock. She didn't want to do this! She'd never considered herself a coward, but being involved in a police capture that could go terribly wrong—or terribly right—sent a bone-deep chill through her. She went over everything that Kyle had told her for the hundredth time.

She was to stand at the end of the dock, and signal with the flashlight to tell Budge she was there. This would also alert the waiting federal cruisers that she was in position, and when Budge brought his boat in to shore to pick her up, they would follow him in and cut off his escape.

It sounded simple enough, she thought, but her eyes anxiously searched the empty beach. Where was Kyle? Her steps faltered. What if he wasn't close enough to protect her if something went wrong? He had assured her that once he glimpsed Budge's boat pulling in at the dock, he'd alert the waiting officers to move in.

The moon went behind a cloud as she approached the boathouse and dock. She slowed to a stop as if her feet refused to carry her any farther. As she stood there, her ears strained to hear some faint assurance that she was not alone in the shadowy darkness, but only the sloshing of water against the pilings of the dock broke the stillness of the night.

She fought the sensation of being all alone at the edge of some dark abyss as her eyes searched the watery darkness. Even when a sliver of moonlight came through the clouds and struck the water, she couldn't see anything but rising and falling surf. The boathouse loomed on one side, and Joseph's fishing boat rocked in the water near the boat slip.

Biting her lip nervously, she slowly walked to the edge of the pier. She set down the carrier and her fingers trembled as she took out the flashlight.

''Hello, sweetheart.'' Budge's whisper was like a clanging gong in her ears.

She swung around, gasping as the flashlight dropped from her hands and clattered on the dock.

With a soft laugh, Budge Gordon stood up in Joseph's fishing boat.

She was too stunned to do anything but stare at him.

Budge was here! Hiding in Joseph's boat!

No, it couldn't be! Kyle's men were waiting for him to bring his boat to shore. Before she could find her voice, he was on the dock beside her.

He'll know I'm not Jill.

Even in the shadowy darkness, she expected him to search her face, or put his hands on her hair, or even pull her close to feel her body once again.

He didn't do any of these things. Without any scrutiny, he accepted the burnished honey-red hair, familiar makeup and the tight pink shorts outfit as his wife's. "We have to get out of here," he said hurriedly as he grabbed her arm.

"No! No!" she gasped and tried to pull away.

"Shut up, Jill, for God's sake!" Manhandling her, he shoved her into the boat with such force that she lost her footing and went down on her knees. Then he dropped the baby carrier beside her, and started the outboard engine.

"We're out of here."

She yelled then, as loudly as she could, from the bottom of the boat, but the cry was drowned in the roar of the engine.

KYLE HAD SEEN her slowly disappear into the darkness of the dock, and he waited for the beam of a flashlight to stab across the water. What was keeping her? He thought he could make out her slender form at the end of the dock, but flickering shadows from the cloudy sky were deceiving. Why didn't she signal Budge to come in and get her? The patrol boats were waiting.

When he heard a faint cry that could have been a nightbird's call, he stiffened, his ears straining to hear any sound coming from the dock. Almost immediately, the sound of a boat's engine hit him like a bolt of thunder.

Someone was taking out Joseph's fishing boat.

Budge!

Scrambling over rocks and thick sea grass, he crossed the beach at a dead run and reached the dock's end just in time to see the spray from a disappearing boat.

Pulling out his phone, he cried, "He's got her! He's about a hundred yards out in a white fishing cruiser. Close in! Close in!"

A fury that was born out of raw fear stabbed at him. Why had he put her life in danger? He knew that she meant more to him than his own life. Nothing mattered more now than her safety. Nothing!

Ashley! Ashley! What would Budge do when he found out he'd been tricked by the wrong twin?

LIGHT BEAMS from waiting boats suddenly came out of the darkness and shot across the water. As Budge swore and sent the boat in a zigzag pattern, Ashley struggled to her feet and lurched to the side of the boat. One thought hammered at her.

Get out before the boat gets too far from the shore!

At that moment, Budge made another sharp turn that put him in a direct line with an outcropping of rocks that narrowed his passage out to sea.

Ashley didn't have time to weigh the situation. She dove over the edge of the boat just seconds before Budge failed to maneuver the speeding boat past the rocky reef. The sound of splintering timbers and crushing metal filled the air.

The turbulence of the water rose like a tidal wave, pulling Ashley into its depths. As she fought her way to the surface amid debris and swirling water, she drew on her strengths as a seasoned swimmer. She could see lights bobbing on the shore, twice as far away as she ever had swum before.

I can make it. I can make it.

Striking out with firm, strong strokes, she cut

through the water, stopping now and again to make certain that her course was true. The beach was dark when she dragged herself out of the water and threw herself down on the wet sand, muscles aching, gasping for breath.

She didn't know how long she lay there, half unconscious from total exhaustion. When a sudden warmth aroused her, she knew without question whose arms were holding her close. As his tender hands brushed the wet tendrils from her face, and his lips warmed hers with soft, loving kisses, she allowed herself a blissful detachment from all that had gone on before.

As Kyle held her in his arms, he knew that he'd never put her in danger again. He'd spend his life protecting her if she'd have him. This assignment was over. By some miracle Budge had been thrown free of the boat and rocks. Justice would have its day, thanks to Ashley's bravery.

When he'd thought she'd been lost, he had nearly died himself. Never, never had he dreamed that love could be so powerful. "I love you, love you, love you," he whispered as if he had to make up for all the time they'd wasted pretending to be other people.

Epilogue

Kyle was granted an extended leave from the Bureau after the successful completion of his assignment. As he and Ashley spent time together, free to be themselves, they were assured that the love that they had for each other was deep and enduring. When he asked Ashley to be Mrs. Kyle Lawrence, she lovingly accepted.

As expected, Budge had been willing to testify against Hugo for a lesser sentence, and the millionaire was convicted of game fixing and illegal gambling rackets that he had pursued for years. There was enough evidence against Rudy Dietz to charge him as an accessory, and he followed his boss to jail.

Pamela and Benny's parents had returned home immediately upon Hugo's arrest, and had taken up residence in the house. When Ashley explained to them about the nanny switch, and the reasons for it, they were more than willing to give Jill the job as year-round companion to the children. They offered housing in the cottage for Davie and her, which she gratefully accepted, realizing after what had happened that she needed to put her life on a different course for herself and her son.

Both children took to the new Jilly without any problem and decided that having two look-alike nannies was great stuff.

Kyle decided to apply for a position with the Colorado branch of the Federal Bureau of Investigation. The couple now resided in a lovely rustic home in the foothills of the Rocky Mountains.

Ashley had continued her professional career, up to now, that is. Because she'd just discovered that the romantic nights and passionate embraces had given them a surprise package.

"Are you sure?" she had asked the doctor in utter amazement.

He nodded. "You're going to be a mother." Then he'd smiled and added, "It appears to be twins."

Psst...

has an even *bigger* secret—

but it's ***confidential***

till September 2001!

HARLEQUIN®
INTRIGUE®

43
Light St.

has been *the* address for outstanding
romantic suspense for more than a decade!
Now REBECCA YORK* blasts the hinges
off the front door with a new trilogy—
MINE TO KEEP.

Look for these great stories on the corner of
heart-stopping romance and breathtaking suspense!

THE MAN FROM TEXAS
August 2001

NEVER ALONE
October 2001

LASSITER'S LAW
December 2001

COME ON OVER...
WE'LL KEEP THE LIGHTS ON.

Available at your favorite retail outlet.

*Ruth Glick writing as Rebecca York

HARLEQUIN®
Makes any time special ®

Visit us at www.eHarlequin.com   HILIGHTST

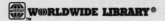

Harlequin truly does make any time special. . . . This year we are celebrating weddings in style!

A Walk Down the Aisle
WEDDING CELEBRATION

To help us celebrate, we want you to tell us how wearing the Harlequin wedding gown will make your wedding day special. As the grand prize, Harlequin will offer one lucky bride the chance to "Walk Down the Aisle" in the Harlequin wedding gown!

There's more...

For her honeymoon, she and her groom will spend five nights at the **Hyatt Regency Maui.** As part of this five-night honeymoon at the hotel renowned for its romantic attractions, the couple will enjoy a candlelit dinner for two in Swan Court, a sunset sail on the hotel's catamaran, and duet spa treatments.

A HYATT RESORT AND SPA

Maui • Molokai • Lanai

To enter, please write, in, 250 words or less, how wearing the Harlequin wedding gown will make your wedding day special. The entry will be judged based on its emotionally compelling nature, its originality and creativity, and its sincerity. This contest is open to Canadian and U.S. residents only and to those who are 18 years of age and older. There is no purchase necessary to enter. Void where prohibited. See further contest rules attached. Please send your entry to:

Walk Down the Aisle Contest

In Canada	In U.S.A.
P.O. Box 637	P.O. Box 9076
Fort Erie, Ontario	3010 Walden Ave.
L2A 5X3	Buffalo, NY 14269-9076

You can also enter by visiting www.eHarlequin.com
Win the Harlequin wedding gown and the vacation of a lifetime!
The deadline for entries is October 1, 2001.

HARLEQUIN®
Makes any time special ®

PHWDACONT1

HARLEQUIN WALK DOWN THE AISLE TO MAUI CONTEST 1197
OFFICIAL RULES
NO PURCHASE NECESSARY TO ENTER

1. To enter, follow directions published in the offer to which you are responding. Contest begins April 2, 2001, and ends on October 1, 2001. Method of entry may vary. Mailed entries must be postmarked by October 1, 2001, and received by October 8, 2001.

2. Contest entry may be, at times, presented via the Internet, but will be restricted solely to residents of certain geographic areas that are disclosed on the Web site. To enter via the Internet, if permissible, access the Harlequin Web site (www.eHarlequin.com) and follow the directions displayed online. Online entries must be received by 11:59 p.m. E.S.T. on October 1, 2001.

    In lieu of submitting an entry online, enter by mail by hand-printing (or typing) on an 8½" x 11" plain piece of paper, your name, address (including zip code), Contest number/name and in 250 words or fewer, why winning a Harlequin wedding dress would make your wedding day special. Mail via first-class mail to: Harlequin Walk Down the Aisle Contest 1197, (in the U.S.) P.O. Box 9076, 3010 Walden Avenue, Buffalo, NY 14269-9076, (in Canada) P.O. Box 637, Fort Erie, Ontario L2A 5X3, Canada.

    Limit one entry per person, household address and e-mail address. Online and/or mailed entries received from persons residing in geographic areas in which Internet entry is not permissible will be disqualified.

3. Contests will be judged by a panel of members of the Harlequin editorial, marketing and public relations staff based on the following criteria:

    * Originality and Creativity—50%
    * Emotionally Compelling—25%
    * Sincerity—25%

    In the event of a tie, duplicate prizes will be awarded. Decisions of the judges are final.

4. All entries become the property of Torstar Corp. and will not be returned. No responsibility is assumed for lost, late, illegible, incomplete, inaccurate, nondelivered or misdirected mail or misdirected e-mail, for technical, hardware or software failures of any kind, lost or unavailable network connections, or failed, incomplete, garbled or delayed computer transmission or any human error which may occur in the receipt or processing of the entries in this Contest.

5. Contest open only to residents of the U.S. (except Puerto Rico) and Canada, who are 18 years of age or older, and is void wherever prohibited by law; all applicable laws and regulations apply. Any litigation within the Province of Quebec respecting the conduct or organization of a publicity contest may be submitted to the Régie des alcools, des courses et des jeux for a ruling. Any litigation respecting the awarding of a prize may be submitted to the Régie des alcools, des courses et des jeux only for the purpose of helping the parties reach a settlement. Employees and immediate family members of Torstar Corp. and D. L. Blair, Inc., their affiliates, subsidiaries and all other agencies, entities and persons connected with the use, marketing or conduct of this Contest are not eligible to enter. Taxes on prizes are the sole responsibility of winners. Acceptance of any prize offered constitutes permission to use winner's name, photograph or other likeness for the purposes of advertising, trade and promotion on behalf of Torstar Corp., its affiliates and subsidiaries without further compensation to the winner, unless prohibited by law.

6. Winners will be determined no later than November 15, 2001, and will be notified by mail. Winners will be required to sign and return an Affidavit of Eligibility form within 15 days after winner notification. Noncompliance within that time period may result in disqualification and an alternative winner may be selected. Winners of trip must execute a Release of Liability prior to ticketing and must possess required travel documents (e.g. passport, photo ID) where applicable. Trip must be completed by November 2002. No substitution of prize permitted by winner. Torstar Corp. and D. L. Blair, Inc., their parents, affiliates, and subsidiaries are not responsible for errors in printing or electronic presentation of Contest, entries and/or game pieces. In the event of printing or other errors which may result in unintended prize values or duplication of prizes, all affected game pieces or entries shall be null and void. If for any reason the Internet portion of the Contest is not capable of running as planned, including infection by computer virus, bugs, tampering, unauthorized intervention, fraud, technical failures, or any other causes beyond the control of Torstar Corp. which corrupt or affect the administration, secrecy, fairness, integrity or proper conduct of the Contest, Torstar Corp. reserves the right, at its sole discretion, to disqualify any individual who tampers with the entry process and to cancel, terminate, modify or suspend the Contest or the Internet portion thereof. In the event of a dispute regarding an online entry, the entry will be deemed submitted by the authorized holder of the e-mail account submitted at the time of entry. Authorized account holder is defined as the natural person who is assigned to an e-mail address by an Internet access provider, online service provider or other organization that is responsible for arranging e-mail address for the domain associated with the submitted e-mail address. **Purchase or acceptance of a product offer does not improve your chances of winning.**

7. Prizes: (1) Grand Prize—A Harlequin wedding dress (approximate retail value: $3,500) and a 5-night/6-day honeymoon trip to Maui, HI, including round-trip air transportation provided by Maui Visitors Bureau from Los Angeles International Airport (winner is responsible for transportation to and from Los Angeles International Airport) and a Harlequin Romance Package, including hotel accomodations (double occupancy) at the Hyatt Regency Maui Resort and Spa, dinner for (2) two at Swan Court, a sunset sail on Kiele V and a spa treatment for the winner (approximate retail value: $4,000); (5) Five runner-up prizes of a $1000 gift certificate to selected retail outlets to be determined by Sponsor (retail value $1000 ea.). Prizes consist of only those items listed as part of the prize. Limit one prize per person. All prizes are valued in U.S. currency.

8. For a list of winners (available after December 17, 2001) send a self-addressed, stamped envelope to: Harlequin Walk Down Aisle Contest 1197 Winners, P.O. Box 4200 Blair, NE 68009-4200 or you may access the www.eHarlequin.com Web site through January 15, 2002.

Contest sponsored by Torstar Corp., P.O. Box 9042, Buffalo, NY 14269-9042, U.S.A.

PHWDACONT2

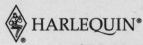